A Perfect Match

Acclaim for Erin Dutton's Fiction

Sequestered Hearts

"*Sequestered Hearts* by first time novelist Erin Dutton, is everything a romance should be. It is teeming with longing, heartbreak, and of course, love...as pure romances go, it is one of the best in print today."—*Just About Write*

Fully Involved

"*Fully Involved* starts with a bang as fire engines race toward a fire at the downtown Hilton Hotel...Dutton literally fills the pages with smoke as she vividly describes the scene. She is equally skilled at showing her readers Reid's feelings of guilt and rage...*Fully Involved* explores the emotional depths of...two very different women. Each woman struggles with loss, change, and the magnetic attraction they have for each other. Their relationship sizzles, flames, and ignites with a page turning intensity. This is an exciting read about two very intriguing women."—*Just About Write*

"Back when Isabel Grant was the tag-along little sister who annoyed them, tomboy Reid Webb and boyhood pal Jimmy Grant considered the girl an intrusion...Years later, Isabel... comes back into Reid's life...and childhood frictions—complicated by Reid's guilty attraction to Isabel—flare into emotional warfare. This being a lesbian romance, no plot points are spoiled by the fact that Reid and Isabel, both stubborn to the core, end up in each other's arms. But Dutton's studied evocation of the macho world of firefighting gives the formulaic story extra oomph—and happily ever after is what a good romance is all about, right?"—*Q Syndicate*

A Place to Rest

"*A Place to Rest* is the story of two women and their contrasting experiences with family. One has a family she rebels against and the other has no family and feels the loss keenly…Erin Dutton has written a novel that is about family dynamics as much as anything…Dutton captures the emotions of…these women very well and engages the reader in the process of hoping that each one is able to overcome her attitudes. Then she surrounds them with secondary characters that fill out the story. The reader gets a chance to think about both what family members can do to each other and what the lack of family means to a person who hasn't had one. The book is listed as a romance, but it goes beyond that."—*Just About Write*

Designed for Love

"*Designed for Love* is…rich in love, romance, and sex. Dutton gives her readers a roller coaster ride filled with sexual thrills and chills as Jillian and Wil battle the attraction between them. *Designed for Love* is the perfect book to curl up with on a cold winter's day."—*Just About Write*

Point of Ignition

"Erin Dutton has given her fans another fast paced story of fire, with both buildings and emotions burning hotly…Dutton has done an excellent job of portraying two women who are each fighting for their own dignity and learning to trust again. The delicate tug of war between the characters is well done as is the dichotomy of boredom and drama faced daily by the firefighters. *Point of Ignition* is a story told well that will touch its readers."—*Just About Write*

By the Author

Visit us at www.boldstrokesbooks.com

A PERFECT MATCH

by

Erin Dutton

2010

A PERFECT MATCH

ISBN 10: 1-60282-145-3
ISBN 13: 978-1-60282-145-3

This Trade Paperback Original Is Published By
Bold Strokes Books, Inc.
P.O. Box 249
Valley Falls, NY 12185

First Edition: April 2010

Credits
Editor: Shelley Thrasher
Production Design: Stacia Seaman
Cover Design By Sheri (graphicartist2020@hotmail.com)
Printed in Canada

Acknowledgments

I was very excited to have the opportunity to write a book about a golfer. Here was another chance to chalk up doing something I love to research. This sport has fostered friendships in my life and has taught me life lessons in patience, accomplishment, and the art of focusing through my frustration.

Before I started playing, I hadn't given much thought to the principles of golf. But I now know there is value to be found in the rules and traditions. Golf is about respect—respecting the game, the course, other players, and most importantly yourself. Trust and honor govern play as you mark your own score on the card with that stubby pencil.

For me, golf is sometimes a way to challenge myself, but it can also be a pleasant way to pass a summer day with a good friend. I hope that my love of the game comes through in this story and these characters.

Writing this book was much the same experience—fun and at times challenging. Thanks to Christina for being there through all phases of this project. Your patience and support made this story possible. I love you.

As always, thanks to Radclyffe, Shelley, and the rest of the wonderful staff of BSB. Their hard work breathes life into the stories in my head.

And thank you to the readers who buy the books, invest in the stories, attend events, and e-mail with their support.

Dedication

To my dad, who introduced me to golf. I will forever cherish the times I've spent next to you in a cart.

Dedication

To my mom, who introduced me to golf. I will forever cherish
the time we spent [...] together [...]

Chapter One

C "an I have your autograph?"

Tiernan O'Shea had just punched the button to call the elevator when she heard the request. An attractive blonde held out a baseball cap and a marker.

"Sure." Tiernan smiled and grabbed the bill of the cap. When the woman didn't let go right away, Tiernan met blue eyes full of interest. Tiernan averted her eyes and the blonde sighed and released it.

"I really love watching you play." Her flirtatious tone hinted that she wasn't ready to give up.

"Thanks." Tiernan carefully kept her voice neutral. People speculated about her sexuality, as they often did about female athletes. In fact, several of her peers on the women's professional golf tour had complained about such stereotypes. Tiernan didn't mind the attention she received from women, but returning it, even if she were free to, would be risky. She signed the hat and handed it back.

"Give 'em hell today," the woman said with a wink.

"I'll try." When the elevator doors slid open, Tiernan stepped inside.

During the short ride to her suite, Tiernan hummed to herself. The Kraft Nabisco Championship was one of her favorite tournaments. Palm Springs was a beautiful place to play, and the coinciding celebrations for Dinah Shore Week drew flocks of women. This year was no different. While she couldn't publicly confirm her own orientation, she could still enjoy surreptitious glances from behind the tinted safety of her sunglasses. But beyond appreciating the scenery, Tiernan envied the women their freedom. She'd heard stories about the parties that took place during the week, but she was far too recognizable to risk attending one of them.

Tiernan surely wasn't the only lesbian on the tour. She wasn't even the first. But though the rumors were well substantiated among players, and the league wouldn't officially forbid it, none competed as openly gay athletes. Tiernan could only guess how the conservative suits at the company that sponsored her would react to a hint of homosexuality.

Tiernan was often torn by a desire to live more honestly. The tour had a large following in the lesbian community, and Tiernan sometimes felt jealous when she witnessed couples strolling among the galleries at tournaments. And though she envied the easy way they interacted with each other, as if they didn't care who might be watching, she'd never have that kind of life. The golfers rarely challenged the unwritten rules about remaining closeted, and she wasn't about to take a chance on losing her endorsement by being photographed at the wrong party. Instead, she played the game and hid her orientation and her relationship.

Tiernan's schedule for the week consisted of multiple practice rounds peppered with interviews and promotional appearances. The tournament sponsored any nightlife she experienced and required her public persona, but the rush of certainty that she would win the tournament outweighed her twinges of resentment that she wasn't able to indulge in the festivities. She exited the elevator and pulled the card key from her back pocket. As she reached her suite she slipped the card into the slot, then pushed the door open.

"Kim," she called as she stepped inside. The main room of

the suite was empty, but through the open bathroom door, she heard the shower running.

She skirted the king-sized bed and opened the closet. After stripping off her T-shirt and tossing it on the bed, she slipped a navy polo bearing a Spin Golf Apparel logo from a hanger. The shower stopped as Tiernan pulled the shirt over her head. She grabbed a white visor, also emblazoned with her sponsor's logo.

"You should go down and have breakfast. The fruit is delicious today." Tiernan strode into the bathroom while tucking the polo into her khaki shorts. She'd been up for hours, having risen early to swim laps in the pool before it got crowded. She'd returned to the room long enough to shower, then went back downstairs for a leisurely breakfast at the café in the courtyard.

The redhead standing in front of the mirror barely glanced at Tiernan as she applied makeup. A plush white towel spanned her torso, ending high on her thigh. Tiernan tried to summon her libido at the sight of her exposed shoulders and the glimpse of cleavage where the towel embraced her ample breasts, but lately Tiernan had been too tired for sex. When she wasn't competing she was either working out or practicing with her new swing coach.

"I don't suppose you have time to go shopping with me this morning."

Tiernan tensed at the sharp tone. She wasn't in the mood for a fight today, but her lover definitely wouldn't like her response. "No, I need to put in some time at the range before I tee off." Over Kim's shoulder Tiernan glanced in the mirror long enough to comb her fingers through short blond hair badly in need of a trim. When she let it get this long, the ends curled against the back of her neck and around her ears.

Kim sighed loudly. "That's not till noon."

"You know I like to get there early." Tiernan favored a relaxed pre-game routine, including plenty of loosening up at the range. She wouldn't consider going shopping with Kim. Even if she managed to drag Kim out of the outlet mall to get back in time, she'd never have the time she needed to center her mind before her round. She moved closer and wrapped an arm around Kim's waist. Hoping to pacify her, she kissed the side of her neck.

"Two hours early?"

Tiernan lifted her head to meet Kim's eyes in the mirror and found them unyielding. Kim traveled with Tiernan under the guise of personal assistant, and though they booked two rooms, they usually shared her suite. Despite Kim's title, she rarely did anything to aid Tiernan professionally. "Do we have to have this fight every week?"

"Apparently, since I have to endure every week being ignored by you."

Tiernan dropped her arms and stepped back. "This is my job. It's not like I'm out running around on you."

"It doesn't matter why. You're not here. I never see you and it doesn't even seem to bother you. Don't you want to spend time with me?"

"This isn't about what I want." Tiernan wanted to defend herself, but she honestly couldn't remember the last time she had made an effort to make time for Kim. So she fell back on her standby excuse. "I have obligations and commitments. If I want to stay in the top of the standings—"

"Fuck the standings. If you want to stay on top of *me*, you'd better start paying me more attention."

Tiernan sighed. Ridiculous as an argument about a shopping trip seemed, this particular battle was much more complex, and Kim had just touched the root of it. She wanted more of Tiernan's time than she was able to give. Even though after nine years on the tour Tiernan had more than proved her talent, a field of women was always at her heels waiting to capitalize on her mistakes. And though twenty-nine was hardly old, Tiernan worked harder every year to stay ahead of the latest young stars. Mentally rationalizing her inattention to their relationship, she realized she was, at least in part, making an excuse. She and Kim hadn't connected in too many months, and her dedication to her career was a convenient distraction. Despite that knowledge, she had just been forced to focus on that very distraction.

"I can't deal with this right now. I'm going to the course to warm up."

Kim didn't respond as she dropped the towel and pulled on a robe from behind the bathroom door.

Tiernan paused only long enough to grab her backpack on her way out. When she would have slammed the door behind her, Kim caught it and followed her down the hallway.

"That's right, walk away, Tiernan. You're damn good at it."

"I'm going to work. But that's not something you'd know anything about." Irritated, Tiernan jabbed the elevator button. The doors slid open and she entered, expecting the argument to end. The doors would close, leaving Kim on the other side, then Tiernan would spend the car ride to the course trying to refocus her energy on her upcoming round.

Instead, Kim stepped inside with her, causing Tiernan to back up and bump the woman standing behind her. She mumbled an apology without looking, only peripherally aware of the car's other occupant.

"Work? Ha. If you think following you around the country acting like I'm nothing but your fucking assistant isn't work, you're out of your mind."

Suddenly hyperaware that they weren't alone, Tiernan spoke quietly. "No one forces you to come along."

"If I didn't, I'd never see you. Between competing and practice, you live and breathe golf. And anyone who's involved with you will always come second."

Tiernan flinched at the way Kim said "involved," making her meaning perfectly clear. The doors opened and Tiernan was horrified to see the lobby filled with press and fans. She gave Kim a hard look and hissed, "Keep your voice down. We can talk about this later."

"I'm so sick of worrying about someone finding out."

"Kim, I said not now."

"How do you expect to ever have a normal relationship when your life is built on lies?"

Tiernan grabbed Kim's arm and tried to usher her out of the elevator, but they'd started to attract attention, and with the crowd pushing closer to hear what was being said, Tiernan didn't have anywhere to go.

Kim jerked her arm out of Tiernan's grasp. "I'm standing here telling you I can't do this anymore and all you can think about is that someone will find out you're a lesbian."

Tiernan stared at her, completely at a loss as to what to say. Panic streaked through her and she glanced around for the nearest exit. The word *lesbian* seemed to echo in the air, and Tiernan felt at least a dozen pairs of eyes on her. Her mind raced for an explanation but Kim wasn't done.

"Show me I'm wrong."

Tiernan recognized reporters from at least three networks and a prominent golf magazine. Her heart pounded so loudly it had to be audible to the people shoving impossibly close. She stood frozen by an ingrained need to protect her secret.

"Tell me our relationship matters to you, without caring who knows." Kim gestured to the crowd around them.

"You don't know what you're asking," Tiernan whispered. This was a bad dream. It had to be. Surely, she would wake up any moment and realize she had been experiencing a horrible nightmare. Maybe she would even tell Kim about it and they would laugh together at her paranoia.

"Yes. Sadly, I do."

Tiernan clenched her teeth to try to control the ache in her throat caused by Kim's devastated expression and the tears rolling freely down her cheeks. Tiernan knew she should do something, but she didn't. Anger at Kim for making a scene mingled with searing hurt at the disappointment dulling the usual luster of Kim's eyes. Kim waited a moment longer, as if giving Tiernan time to choose her. That silent collection of seconds contained an implied ultimatum, yet she couldn't respond. When Kim turned and walked away, Tiernan could almost feel the physical rending of her heart.

Half of the crowd tried to follow Kim, but she was heading for the stairs and had a lead on them. The rest of the reporters pressed closer to Tiernan and began to ask questions.

Tiernan couldn't make sense of their words. She tried desperately to keep her shield up against their rapid-fire shouts. "I—I don't—"

"Excuse me. Let me through." The familiar voice of Brit Dailey, her friend and caddy, rang from the back of the group. "Make room. *Excuse me.*"

In a moment, the small dynamo had shoved through the tight-knit crowd and grabbed Tiernan's elbow. She was nearly six inches shorter than Tiernan, but she took control of the situation with an air of confidence.

"Brit, I can't—"

"Don't say another word. The valet is bringing up the car. Let's get you out of here," Brit said, close to her ear. To the crowd she shouted, "No comment. Make room, please." Her cap of blond ringlets bounced as she led Tiernan through the lobby. She didn't slow her pace at all, leaving anyone in her way no choice but to move.

❖

As the mob followed the two women rushing toward the door, Elena Pilar still stood in front of the elevator doors, shocked at what she'd just witnessed. She had recognized Tiernan O'Shea the moment she'd stepped on the elevator. Anyone even remotely close to professional golf knew who she was. The lean, attractive golfer was a fan favorite and over her career had been the subject of much media coverage.

Up close, Tiernan was even more arresting. Shades of blond and light brown added depth to her thick hair, and her blue eyes were even more expressive, darkening like the churning sea when Tiernan got angry. Comparing Tiernan's height against her own, Elena figured she couldn't be more than five foot six, but her energy filled the elevator, making her seem larger. Her shoulders, which appeared almost too broad for her narrow hips, bunched beneath her polo as she gestured sharply during the confrontation.

As a sports commentator, Elena knew Tiernan O'Shea's game inside and out. In fact, in the past few years, she'd been studying Tiernan, along with the other players on the pro tour, in the hopes that she would someday get assigned to a professional tournament. But she'd never expected to learn so much about Tiernan's personal life. Elena had been startled to see Tiernan step on the elevator and even more shocked when her gorgeous robe-clad companion entered the car behind her. Their angry declarations had piqued Elena's interest. Initially uncomfortable witnessing the exchange, she decided if they wanted it to remain private they shouldn't have brought it into the elevator.

Tiernan O'Shea is a lesbian. The statement continued to circulate in Elena's head. Had she heard wrong? No. The top women's golfer in the world had just been outed, and within the hour the whole world would be talking about her sexuality. By the time Tiernan teed off this afternoon, no one would be looking at the leaderboard.

How would Tiernan get herself under control before her round? Her obvious anger and embarrassment must be interfering with her usual pre-game composure. Today wasn't the first time Elena had studied Tiernan's expressive features. She'd watched Tiernan play many times, though before it had always been on television.

Prior to this week, covering college golf had been Elena's most prestigious job in the four years she'd worked at ASC, a national sports network. A curl of nervousness augmented the excitement she'd been feeling about this week's assignment. She crossed the now-deserted lobby. Nearly the entire hotel was booked with media, golfers and their various entourage of caddies, agents, and coaches, and most had already left for the course. She brought up her daily calendar on her BlackBerry. In less than an hour, she would be standing next to the eighteenth green as the early groups finished their rounds.

She glanced at her watch and plotted out the next sixty minutes. A minute and a half to her rental car in the adjacent parking garage, then, with tournament traffic, eleven minutes to the media entrance at the course. She'd timed her route the day before. Ten minutes in the restroom touching up her makeup and making sure her ebony hair was securely bound in the twist resting against the back of her head. That left thirty-seven minutes to get miked, confer with the booth announcers, and reach her assigned place on the eighteenth green.

During Elena's drive to the course, the scene in the elevator continued to play in her head. Tiernan radiated an overwhelming energy, and just now that force had been decidedly negative. Tiernan's unwillingness, or inability, to conceal the emotions in her cerulean eyes had always intrigued Elena. Winning or losing, Tiernan didn't hold herself back while playing, a quality Elena believed partly responsible for her commercial success. Fans liked a player they felt they knew—they could relate to Tiernan because she openly displayed the same range of jubilation and frustration they associated with the game. Tiernan could never be one of the robotic young athletes the sport seemed to churn out these days.

Elena was curious, not only about how Tiernan would handle the media fallout from the confrontation, but how the league would react. League officials wouldn't want the negative publicity, but Tiernan was the kind of golfer who sold tickets. Yes, this week's tournament just got even more interesting.

CHAPTER TWO

"Son of a bitch," Tiernan muttered, shifting in the soft leather passenger seat of the sedan.

"Calm down," Brit said evenly as she steered into traffic.

"That's all you've got? My life has just been *fucked* and you're telling me to *calm down*."

"Now isn't the time to overreact."

Briefly, it occurred to Tiernan that Brit was only trying to preserve their pre-game routine, but she was angry and embarrassed. "Damn it." Tiernan slammed her fist against the center console and Brit jumped. "This is ridiculous. Wait until I get back tonight. Kim and I are going to have it out. I'll make her little show in the elevator look like afternoon tea."

"I don't think that's a good idea."

Tiernan jerked to face Brit and she flinched. "She outed me because she couldn't control her damn jealousy of my career. Ha. She conveniently forgets it's that same career that pays for her massages and shopping and fancy dinners while I'm on the range practicing my ass off." The more Tiernan replayed their display in the lobby, the angrier she got. Kim was being ungrateful and she had a lot of making up to do if she hoped to repair the damage she'd caused this morning.

"The last thing you need right now is to have someone overhear an argument between the two of you. The tour's PR people will probably have some idea how they want to spin this."

"Spin it?"

"Yes."

Tiernan studied her caddy's profile. Brit had been her best friend since they'd played golf together in college, and Tiernan didn't trust anyone on the course more. When she'd secured her first tour card, her agent had urged her to hire one of the many established professional caddies, but Tiernan refused. Brit knew Tiernan's game, not just club length and putting lines, but the emotional side as well. She knew when to push her as well as when to rein her in.

As they pulled into the drive at Mission Hills Country Club, Tiernan groaned. A flock of reporters clustered around the entrance to the players' parking area like vultures waiting to pick her bones clean.

"I'll pull up to the door," Brit said.

"No. Park in the player lot."

"You can be out and inside before they can get over there. I'll bring your things in later."

"We'll go in just as we did yesterday." The idea of avoiding the scavengers was attractive, but evasion would only delay the inevitable.

Though Tiernan could see Brit's desire to argue in the tightness of her jaw, Brit remained silent as she steered into an open spot. Tiernan took a deep breath and slipped on her sunglasses, then shoved the car door open. She didn't respond to any of the questions that the group of men and women who swarmed toward her were yelling. Instead, she simply grabbed her club bag from the trunk and strode toward the clubhouse. She paid no attention to the reporters in her way, assuming they would either move or get a sharp rap from her bag as she passed. Questions were being hurled at Brit, but neither of them slowed.

Tiernan sighed as they stepped inside, where the reporters were barred from following. Those who had the proper credentials could go onto the course, but media personnel were not allowed inside the clubhouse prior to the day's rounds. Tiernan crossed the lobby, seeking the safety of the locker room where she would only have to endure the curious stares of her fellow competitors.

❖

"Elena, are you in position?" The soft, feminine voice of Elena's producer sounded in her earpiece.

"I'm here." Elena spoke into her microphone.

An island green waited for players at the eighteenth, making it the most picturesque in women's golf and one of Elena's favorites. The area for the spectators and media had been set up just next to the small walk bridge that led to the green. Elena had secured her place as close to the bridge as allowed, so she could be one of the first to interview the players after they completed their round.

Though the first pairings wouldn't arrive here for nearly an hour, the bleachers were already filled to half-capacity. Elena had seen a definite increase in attendance in the past few years. Unfortunately, the rise in fan loyalty didn't translate into more money from the sponsors or more credibility for the league. Women's golf often was still considered second rate in comparison to the men's league.

Most of the sportscasters Elena had met over the years aspired to call men's tournaments, but Elena couldn't be happier to be standing right where she was. After her colleague's sudden illness, Elena had jumped on a late flight from Orlando last night. She'd arrived at the hotel in time to grab a couple hours of sleep before finding herself in the elevator this morning. The regular announcer would recover and return in time for the next tournament. Then Elena would once again be covering college matches. But she was soaking in every moment of this weekend, and she vowed to return to professional golf someday.

"Elena, once the groups get close we'll go to you for their

approach shots and putt reads. David and Bobby will feed you cues from the booth and you just roll with it."

"Got it." Elena adjusted the small black box clipped to her waistband in the small of her back, then smoothed a hand over the lapels of her blazer. She wouldn't appear on camera today. Instead, her role would be strictly auditory, a voice in the background of the play. But though she felt slightly out of her depth, she wanted to appear professional and polished to her colleagues and the spectators around her.

Tiernan stepped outside and immediately reached for the sunglasses resting on the bill of her visor. As she followed the path toward the driving range, she slipped the shades over her eyes, blocking out the sun and the speculative looks from those around her.

"Going to be a scorcher, even for April in California," Brit said as Tiernan approached the practice tee.

"Forecasted highs over ninety-five." Tiernan tugged a glove onto her left hand, then took the club Brit held out.

"Drink plenty of water."

"It's not my first tournament in hot weather, Brit."

"Easy on the attitude. I didn't do anything to you." Brit tossed three balls on the ground in front of Tiernan.

"I know. I'm sorry." Tiernan tapped one ball forward with her clubhead and settled into her stance. "I don't know why I'm letting this get to me."

"I could guess."

"What?" Tiernan knew she sounded snappish but she couldn't shake her ill temper.

"Clearly, this brings back old hurt about your dad."

Tiernan shook her head as if she could deny the truth of Brit's words. "This has nothing to do with him."

"Okay. I'm just say—"

"Well, don't." Tiernan didn't want the shadows of her father's disgrace and her mother's embarrassment at the hands of the media to infuse her warm-up session. But she couldn't chase away the memory of being twelve years old and overhearing the late-night fights about reports of infidelity. She remembered her father, a PGA golfer, telling her mother that the press had fabricated and sensationalized the story.

When she swung her club, her body felt tight and the motion awkward. The obviously mishit ball shot off to the right. Tiernan scowled. She could practically hear the creaking of necks as everyone turned to stare at her.

"Oh, what are you looking at?" When Tiernan snapped at the golfer nearest her, she immediately heard the clicking of several cameras nearby and had to restrain herself from flipping off the media members.

"Tiernan." Brit grabbed her elbow. "We don't have time for this. You tee off in an hour and all this nonsense has already disrupted your routine."

"Nonsense?" Tiernan paused and lowered her voice. "The demise of my relationship is *nonsense?*"

Brit laughed. "Demise? That's a bit melodramatic, don't you think?"

"No. Yes. I don't know."

"Was it really a relationship, anymore?"

"Yes." Tiernan had thought so, but now she was having her doubts. Mostly, she'd been satisfied with her arrangement with Kim. Hadn't she? Looking back she couldn't remember a time when they didn't argue constantly, but there must have been— they must have been happy once. She needed to recall those memories. Then maybe after her round she could find Kim and they would work it out. "It was—is a relationship. And when I get back to the room, Kim and I will talk through things. Maybe I'll take her away somewhere next week."

"You're shooting a television commercial next Thursday. Then Kingsmill is the weekend after that. We need to stick to your training routine."

"After Kingsmill, then." Tiernan looked forward to the tournament in Williamsburg every year. The events leading up to the league play promoted youth golf and raised a ton of money for a number of local charities and public-service organizations.

"We have back-to-back tournaments the following two weekends. Then you're playing in that pro-am in Orlando next month."

"Cancel it. I'm not in the mood to play with some amateur anyway."

"You love those hometown publicity machines. And it's for a good cause."

"Fine. But after that, we're going someplace tropical and private. See what you can find." Tiernan took a tentative test swing but it still didn't feel natural. She needed to restore the balance. "Give me your phone."

"What?"

"Come on. I left mine in the locker room. Give it up." Tiernan ignored Brit's sigh as she handed over her cell. Tiernan flipped it open and dialed the front desk at her hotel. "This is Tiernan O'Shea. Could you have the hotel florist send an expensive arrangement to 407?"

"Certainly, Miss O'Shea." Tiernan heard the soft click of computer keys. "I'm sorry, but the guest in 407 has checked out."

"There must be some mistake. Kim Donovan?"

"Yes. Ms. Donovan checked out this morning."

"Are you sure?"

"Yes, ma'am. I took care of it myself." When Tiernan didn't respond, the clerk continued. "Will there be anything else?"

"No. Thank you." She snapped the phone shut and handed it back to Brit. "She left."

"Without telling you?"

"Obviously." She took two steps away, then back. She needed to think—needed to pace, but didn't have any place to go. Suddenly the other golfers, tournament employees, and media representatives seemed to be closing in on her. "I need some air."

"You're outside."

She ignored Brit as she headed for the clubhouse.

"Hey, you haven't even warmed up yet." Brit followed her, and when Tiernan jerked to a stop as she passed through the bar, Brit ran into her back.

"What the hell?"

Kim's face filled the television screen behind the bar, her expression one of irritation as she tried to push her way past several reporters. As the camera zoomed out, Tiernan could tell Kim was at the airport.

"Miss Donovan, what is the nature of your relationship with Tiernan O'Shea?"

"Were you lovers?"

"How long have you had a sexual relationship with Tiernan O'Shea?"

The questions were shouted rapid-fire. Even if Kim had wanted to, she wouldn't have time to reply.

"Miss Donovan, can you confirm rumors that you were one in a string of women Tiernan O'Shea is involved with?"

The last inquiry commanded Kim's attention, and she stared levelly at the reporter who'd asked.

"Oh, shit," Tiernan muttered. "Don't do it."

Kim turned her head, and when she found the camera she looked straight into it. "I have been in a committed *monogamous* relationship with Tiernan O'Shea for seven years, which I agreed to keep secret because women's golf isn't ready for an honest-to-God dyke. Instead of letting young girls have a real role model, they encourage players to conceal their true selves."

"Damn." Tiernan felt every pair of eyes in the bar shift to her.

"Let's go." Brit grabbed Tiernan's arm and steered her toward the restroom down the hall. Once inside, she flipped the lock, barring anyone from following them.

Tiernan paced in front of the row of sinks, unable to disentangle the thoughts crowding her head.

Brit stepped in front of Tiernan. "You need to forget about all this."

"How exactly am I supposed to do that?" Tiernan tugged off her visor and shoved a hand through her hair. "I need to go to the airport."

"You don't have time."

"I've got an hour and a half."

"Yes, and with traffic it's at least forty-five minutes round trip. If you miss your tee time, you're disqualified."

"So what?" Tiernan flopped down on a bench in front of the lockers.

Brit grabbed Tiernan's shoulders. "If you think about this logically for a minute, you'll see that you need to stay here and concentrate on widening your lead. That's our goal for today. When we get back to the hotel tonight, you'll call Kim and smooth things over. She's mad and probably needs time to cool down."

Tiernan took several deep breaths and forced herself to listen to Brit's words.

"You're right," she said too firmly, though not totally convinced. This wasn't the first time Kim had been mad at her. Tiernan had returned from several rounds before to find Kim stewing in her own hotel room, but she'd never left. Tiernan could usually placate her with expensive room service and an evening to themselves.

❖

"Now, let's go to Dakota Mayer at the practice tees where the leaders are warming up." The voice of Bobby Lambert, one of the desk announcers, in Elena's ear drew her attention. Down the fairway, she could see the first pairing approaching and mentally readied for her upcoming cue.

"Bobby, the drama over here rivals that of the players already on the course." As Dakota spoke, Elena pictured his thick blond hair neatly tamed into a wave over his forehead, his tanned face, and chemically whitened teeth. His jacket and tie matched just a little too well, and overall he projected an image of trying too hard. He wanted to work a PGA tournament so badly that he didn't care if his co-workers and producer knew that he considered his current post merely a stepping stone.

"Well, what is going on over there, Dakota?" Bobby sounded far too interested in dishing dirt.

"Tiernan O'Shea looked visibly upset when she came to the practice tee just fifteen minutes ago. She quickly retreated to the locker room with her caddy. But apparently Dailey was able to calm the notoriously emotional golfer because they've reemerged, O'Shea with a resolved expression."

"Certainly if anyone can calm O'Shea down, it's her caddy. Brit Dailey practically makes a living interpreting O'Shea's moods. Don't you think, David?"

Elena had watched the interplay between Bobby and his counterpart, David Sands, often enough to imagine Bobby's expression as he turned to the man sitting next to him. Both men were retired pro golfers and well respected in the profession.

"There's never a dull tournament when Tiernan is playing," David said. "But for now, let's focus on the course. The first pairing is approaching the final hole. Elena, what does it look like out there?"

Elena took one last quick glance at her notes about the two golfers in the fairway in front of her. "David, these two are definitely not chasing the lead. But for Gokey, a birdie on this hole will cap off a great round, finishing at eight under for the day. Sanchez, however, barely made the cut after a disastrous round yesterday. She probably just wants to put this tournament behind her and start looking to the next one."

"What do their approach shots look like?"

"Gokey's got a nice little pitch from the fairway onto this big island green. She has a lob wedge in hand and will try to stick it as close as possible." Elena paused as the golfer set up, then took an easy half swing and practically floated the ball into the air. "This looks good." The ball hit the ground just a foot from the hole, then hopped twice toward it and stopped inside six inches. "That's an incredible shot, David. Gokey will tap that in for a birdie, finishing a stellar round today."

When the announcers cut away to get an update on another pairing, Elena breathed in relief. She wasn't a rookie. For six years, she'd been behind a sports desk and on camera at various events. She hadn't expected the nervousness churning in her stomach and making her palms damp. Fighting the urge to wipe her hands on her skirt, she took another deep breath and adjusted her earpiece. *You can do this.* Conscious of her microphone, she avoided speaking the reminder out loud. Despite how she actually felt, she would project an air of confidence.

CHAPTER THREE

"How are you feeling, Tiernan?"

"Have you spoken to Kim Donovan?"

"Any predictions for today's round?"

"Are you and Kim through?"

Tiernan used every ounce of her willpower to ignore the questions shouted at her as she exited the clubhouse and walked to the first tee. Once there she would have a reprieve. Tour officials wouldn't allow the press to harass a player during her round.

"Don't listen," Brit said quietly, as she matched Tiernan's strides.

"Easier said than done." Any progress Tiernan had made in getting focused was quickly slipping away.

Tiernan stepped into the semicircular clearing of people waiting to watch the players tee off. Her tee time was announced, each name followed by applause, and she shook hands with the player she was paired with today, an up-and-coming rookie named Regina Paine. Regina was currently in second place, six shots behind Tiernan's score.

Tiernan slipped her sunglasses over her eyes and tuned out the noise around her. She focused instead on the familiar sensation of being on the tee at the start of a tournament. She tilted her head down and the sun quickly warmed the back of her neck. Though the grounds crew had been out at sunrise, the smell of fresh-cut grass still lingered. Staring down the fairway, she zeroed in on the flag and visualized the hole. She would place her first shot in the center of the fairway and her second on the green, leaving her with one putt to start her round with a birdie.

Tiernan got a handful of tees from her bag and slipped them into her pocket. She grabbed two balls and rotated them in her hand, their dimpled surfaces rubbing soothingly against her palm. Brit pulled out the driver, removed the headcover, and handed it to her. After Tiernan glanced once more down the fairway and played the hole in her mind, she teed up a ball and settled into her stance. She took another couple of seconds to sight her target before she swung.

A camera clicked in the middle of her backswing, the soft opening and closing of a shutter that most people wouldn't even register. But in Tiernan's unfocused mental state, the sound was enough to put a hitch in her swing. A murmur rippled through the crowd as she hooked the ball into the trees on the left side of the fairway.

Tiernan handed her club back to Brit, smothering a curse. As she strode wordlessly down the fairway, she remapped her plan for this hole. First shot went far left. Second shot?

"Damn it," Tiernan muttered as she reached her ball. She'd driven it right into the middle of a cluster of low-limbed trees. She didn't have a good view of the flag through the trees, but there was a break in them to her right. Her only options were to go under the limbs or laterally into the fairway beside her.

"Just stick it out in the fairway," Brit said, after she'd also assessed the lie of the ball. "You can be on the green in three and one putt for par."

Tiernan bent to study the situation from under the canopy of the trees. "I can probably keep it low enough."

"If you go that low, you'll never clear that bunker. You're still looking at three shots to get there."

Brit was right. The three sand traps that surrounded the first green prevented a low-trajectory shot from reaching the putting surface. Tiernan nodded and shifted to line up for a punch shot into the fairway. She easily put the ball out in the center and handed her club back to Brit.

As Tiernan walked across the fairway, she watched Regina strike her ball, sending it in a perfect arc. It landed on the green and stopped about twenty feet from the hole. Tiernan needed to stick her shot closer if she hoped to sink it with only one putt.

She stood over her ball, club in hand, ready to swing, but suddenly Kim's face flashed in her head. She saw Kim's look of disappointment just before she walked away, and all Tiernan felt was guilt. Kim had asked her to acknowledge their relationship. And at that point, Tiernan had nothing to lose by doing so because she'd just been effectively outed anyway. She couldn't possibly deny she was a lesbian now. But she hadn't said the words Kim needed to hear, and her inability to do so hadn't been completely out of fear. She half realized that she no longer felt them. She'd stayed with Kim out of habit and convenience.

Tiernan stepped back and looked down the fairway again. She stared at the flag, flapping in the slight left-to-right wind.

"Tiernan?" Brit's voice cut through the muddle of thoughts in her head.

She shook her head and moved over her ball once more. Her mind was clear when she swung, but she put the ball up a little higher than she wanted to and didn't get the distance she needed. It fell on the edge of the green, in the fringe of slightly longer grass, and rolled only a few inches.

"All right, we're putting, at least," Brit said as they approached the green. A crowd of people pressed close, restrained only by the yellow rope strung through posts driven in the ground for this weekend's tournament.

"I'm twenty feet away, maybe more."

Brit set Tiernan's golf bag down and pulled out her putter. Tiernan took the club and went to her ball without waiting for

Brit to follow. She visualized the track of the ball to the hole, watching for any rises or dips along the way that might affect the direction of her putt.

While taking an easy practice stroke with the putter, she tried to chase Kim's face out of her head once again. Then she hit the ball with carefully controlled speed and watched it follow the line toward the hole she'd envisioned. But when it got within two feet, it veered slightly left and rolled past the hole. Tiernan closed her eyes for a second, then crossed to where her ball had stopped and bent to replace it with a small circular marker so it wouldn't hinder Regina's putt. After Regina's ball stopped short of the hole, they each took a turn tapping in the remaining distance.

"Dropped a stroke," Tiernan muttered as she walked off the green. Regina had made par, putting her ball in with four shots, while Tiernan's five shots left her with a bogey. Tiernan's lead had just shortened by one.

"It's only the first hole. We'll get it back." Brit's confidence was reassuring.

Tiernan chose to believe her. There was a lot of golf left to play, and if she could keep her head together, this tournament was still hers to win.

❖

"Tiernan O'Shea finishes that hole with another bogey. She's clinging to a one-shot lead over Regina Paine and, David, the way she's playing, I'm not sure how long she can hold on." Resignation was evident in Dakota's voice. He'd given up on Tiernan, for good reason. Tiernan's lead had slipped away. But Elena thought he might be counting her out far too early.

The first four holes had been disastrous for Tiernan, and she had lost most of her lead there. Regina wasn't making a strong move to take over, but unless Tiernan could turn it around, Regina only needed to play consistent par golf.

"Dakota, what's going on down there? Has she simply let the drama with the press get to her today?"

Elena rolled her eyes at David's question. Would he ask the same question of a male golfer?

"She very well could have." Dakota played into the angle. "She seems distracted and uncomfortable on the course."

Bobby jumped in. "But certainly, she's faced adversity before. Last year, she came back from a four-shot deficit at the U.S. Open to win the whole thing."

"In ten-mile-per-hour wind," David added.

"That was an impressive round. But do you remember how intensely focused she was that day? You could read the concentration in her face. I don't see that today. She's distracted and short-tempered, and not doing a very good job hiding it."

Dakota didn't hold back and Elena detected a note of satisfaction in his voice. But it wasn't the first time she'd heard one of the guys seeming to enjoy the difficulties of one of the golfers.

❖

"You're rushing your shots."

"What the fuck difference does it make?" Tiernan growled. She'd forsaken her normal pre-shot routine three holes ago. She was standing in the middle of the eighteenth fairway at the end of what was no doubt the worst round of her professional career. Regina Paine had taken over the lead on the fourteenth hole and Tiernan's game had steadily declined, leaving her three shots behind. Panic raced along her spine and pooled in her sweating palms. She wiped her hands on her thighs.

"Slow down and breathe."

Tiernan took the six iron Brit held out. She rolled her shoulders and tried to force herself to calm down, but she couldn't shake her growing frustration. She'd begun her day with three consecutive bogeys and a double-bogey. She'd started the back nine only one shot ahead and needing to birdie as many holes as she could. After eight holes and not one birdie, Tiernan thought she was living a nightmare.

She couldn't get the scene with Kim out of her head or stop thinking about what her next move should be. Certainly Kim expected her to come home and beg her to take her back. It's what she'd done before. But this time was different, not only because of the very public nature of their argument, but because now Tiernan wasn't sure she wanted to go back.

She stared down the fairway at the flag, which taunted her with a fluttering wave. The eighteenth was the longest par five on the course. Tiernan had driven the ball perfectly in the center of the fairway, a straight shot that got a generous amount of roll after it landed.

"Give me the three wood." Tiernan passed the six iron back to Brit and waited for her to hand over the one she'd requested.

"This is what you need." Brit still held the club.

"I'm not laying up."

"You can't carry that water from here."

The island green loomed 260 yards away. She would be foolish to risk putting one in the water. But the high from her perfect drive surged through her, nourishing a tiny bit of hope that she could pull off something spectacular to end this horrible day.

"I've hit that before."

"Yeah, when it didn't matter. This isn't the time to be trying this shot."

"What better time?" Tiernan reached around Brit and yanked the three wood from her bag. "I can eagle this hole."

"It won't give you the lead."

"I'll be within one."

Brit didn't even consider Tiernan's argument before shaking her head. "It's too risky. You need to play safe. We'll start fresh tomorrow. There's still plenty of time to get your lead back."

Tiernan shook her head and, without waiting for any further argument, turned away. She tried to ignore the huff of disapproval from over her shoulder as she set up for her shot. Shifting her weight almost imperceptibly as she stood there for a moment, she tried to calm herself. Edginess and discomfort almost made her step back but she forced her swing anyway.

"Damn it." A knot of dread tightened in her stomach as she realized she wouldn't carry the water. The splash seconds later was followed by a groan from the gallery of fans nearby.

"Don't throw it," Brit hissed from behind her.

Tiernan squeezed the grip of the club so hard her knuckles ached and reminded herself that the crowd around her was no doubt waiting for her reaction.

"Give me another ball."

"No."

Brit, give me—"

"No." Brit strode forward and stood nose to nose with Tiernan. When she spoke her voice was low but hard. "You are not pulling this fucking *Tin Cup* shit on me now. You go up there and take your drop so you can try to save par." Brit shouldered the bag and walked away, leaving Tiernan no choice but to follow.

Dread crept through Tiernan as she trudged up to the edge of the water, but she struggled not to show it. She'd had a chance, had made that shot before and believed she could do it again. Since the age of three when her father first put a golf club in her hand, Tiernan had never counted anything out. She'd spent her childhood around professional golfers, making shots that they bet she couldn't make, and each time her father swelled with pride, Tiernan's confidence grew exponentially. She pushed her body and her mind, and often the outcome was more than even she had thought possible.

Finish this strong. Tiernan mentally coached herself for only a second before she lowered her head and settled over the ball.

❖

Standing in the media area, Elena watched Tiernan pitch her ball onto the green from the other side of the water. The short shot landed on the green and left her with less than six feet to putt. Elena realized she'd been holding her breath and released it slowly. Tiernan had a makeable putt and could end her day with par. The score would place her in no better position mathematically going into the final round, but Elena suspected she would feel marginally better than had she made another bogey.

Tiernan and Brit crossed the bridge to the green together. Their heads were bent as they conversed, and though Elena couldn't tell what was being said, she suspected Brit was delivering a pep talk. *Sink this putt and put today behind you. Go into tomorrow with a positive mindset.* It's what Elena would tell her. But she doubted Tiernan needed the sentiments. Though Tiernan had played professionally for only nine years, she'd been around the game all of her life, so no doubt she knew how to recover from a hard day.

Because Regina's ball was farther away, she putted first and left her ball six inches short of the hole. Tiernan gestured for her to tap it in and she did so for par.

Tiernan crouched to study the line of her putt and Elena squinted, trying to see Tiernan's eyes. She wished she could read the emotion in them, the thoughts behind them, at that moment.

"Elena, how does it look?" David asked, cuing her to evaluate the shot.

"David, she's got a good break from right to left, and it's downhill, so judging the speed is crucial here." Elena spoke quietly, nearly whispering so she wouldn't distract the golfers. The crowd in the bleachers became impossibly silent as well, all aware of the etiquette required around the golf green.

Tiernan stroked her putt smoothly and the ball rolled forward, curving just as Elena had predicted. But Tiernan had allowed for the break and it dropped into the cup. Tomorrow, she would start the final day of the tournament three shots behind Regina Paine.

"O'Shea is on her way off the green." The cue from the

booth to Elena's earpiece was unnecessary. She'd already caught sight of Tiernan striding toward the cluster of media personnel surrounding Elena.

Tiernan's caddy hurried to keep up, and though Elena couldn't hear what she was saying, her expression was tight and her lips moved rapidly. Tiernan's hushed responses were equally terse. The crowd of reporters surged forward and surrounded the pair, bumping one another as they fought for position. Shutters snapped and course etiquette disappeared as reporters began shouting questions.

"Tiernan, where's Kim?"

"Are you two still together?"

"How long have you been a lesbian?"

Elena nearly chuckled at that last one—as if Tiernan had just decided one day that being a lesbian might be a good idea.

"Tiernan, what are your plans to prepare for tomorrow's round?" Elena shouted one of the few golf-related questions.

Uncharacteristically, Tiernan ignored them all. In the past, Elena had gotten the impression that Tiernan viewed the press as a necessary part of professional golf and usually stopped to answer the obligatory questions before going into the tent to sign her scorecard. Today, however, Tiernan continued forward with no response. The media refused to be ignored, though, and as Tiernan moved toward the tent they closed in on her. Elena was swept up in the crowd, jostled among the reporters that pressed around Tiernan and her caddy.

"Make room, please," Brit Dailey shouted above the questions peppering the air. "Let us through."

No one retreated. Instead they seemed to push even closer. Elena fought against the wave of people but suddenly found herself near Tiernan, separated from her only by one persistent man with a camera. When Tiernan would have forced her way past him, the man reached out and grabbed her arm. Tiernan whipped around, jerked her arm away, and shoved him.

Elena didn't react quickly enough to avoid the heavy camera

in his hand as he flailed his arms in an attempt to regain his balance. Pain, sharp and hot, streaked through her left cheekbone and temple, and she stumbled back several steps. Instinctively, she covered her face with her hand, and when she pulled it down, blood stained her palm. Through blurred vision, she saw Tiernan disappear through the crowd now closing in around Elena to check on her. Tiernan didn't look back.

Chapter Four

The steady whir of the treadmill belt, the rhythmic slap of Tiernan's sneakers against its deck, and her labored breathing were the only sounds in the darkened hotel gym. Tiernan glanced down at the display and pushed the button to increase her speed. She'd been running for over thirty minutes, and despite the sweat dripping down her body, she was unable to cleanse herself of the day's stress. So she swiped her forearm across her forehead and edged the speed up a little further. Her legs churned, working to keep up with the spinning belt, and her lungs burned as she sucked in air. But she didn't slow, even when she heard the glass door behind her open.

"What are you doing?" Brit asked as she crossed to Tiernan's side.

"Running," Tiernan said, between panting breaths.

"Obviously. You're not wearing yourself out, are you? We've got a lot of work to do tomorrow."

Tiernan sighed and slowed her pace. "I need to clear my head."

"Find another way." Brit reached across the console and stopped the treadmill.

As Tiernan stepped down, Brit tossed her a towel. She paced the floor between rows of ellipticals and stationary bikes, then paused to stretch her legs. They would be tight tomorrow, but nothing a little extra warm-up wouldn't fix. In the early days of her relationship with Kim, Tiernan could always count on a particularly athletic round of sex to keep her relaxed between rounds. They had clashed on some things from day one, but sex was the one area where they never had any problems.

"Did you try to call Kim?" Brit asked, as if reading her mind.

Tiernan nodded. "She didn't answer."

"She will. After you finish tomorrow, we can head home and you can patch it up."

She and Kim needed to have a conversation, but truthfully, she hadn't expected her to pick up the phone. "That's the thing, Brit. I'm not sure I want to stay with her." Tiernan crossed to a bench against the wall and picked up a bottle of water.

"You've been together for seven years. Are you sure this is the end?"

"We were twenty-two when we got together. Just kids." Tiernan sat on the bench and slouched against the wall.

"Were? You know, compared to some people, you aren't exactly an old lady." At thirty-three, four years older than Tiernan, Brit already considered herself middle-aged. She said she'd packed more into her first three decades than most people did their whole lives. A natural daredevil, she'd gone skydiving, jumped off cliffs in Mexico, taken an African safari, and snowboarded all over the world, and all of that while keeping the same grueling schedule as Tiernan.

"These past nine years have really taken it out of me." Tiernan pressed the water bottle to her forehead, enjoying the cool plastic against her still-heated skin.

"You're not thinking of slowing down, are you? We're going to have a great season. You're in the best shape of your life." Brit plopped down beside Tiernan.

"And I'm working my ass off to stay that way. All I'm saying is, Kim and I don't want the same things anymore."

"Yeah, *she* wants to shop and spend your money."

"Ah, your true feelings are coming out." Tiernan laughed. She'd always suspected Brit didn't really like Kim, but tolerated her because she thought Kim made Tiernan happy.

Brit laughed in return.

"*She* wants a relationship, out in the open. Seriously, I can't be that person. I don't want to be some poster-girl lesbian. I don't want my life lived out in front of the media." The negative effect of press coverage on her parents' relationship had scarred her in ways she had always been afraid to examine.

"You might not have a choice now, whether you like it or not. Now that you pretty much are out, do you think the two of you can sort through things?" Brit asked.

"I don't know. Obviously that wasn't our only issue. She's never thought I made enough time for her. That's what we were arguing about this morning."

"That's not likely to change."

"No. I don't plan to retire from golf any time soon. Even if I cut back on training, I suspect it would never be enough. I know she was angry in the elevator, so I guess I understand her outburst in the lobby. But, knowing how I feel about going public, I can't believe she confirmed it in the airport. I mean, did you see her face? She knew exactly how I would react when I saw that scene."

Brit sat silently, though it seemed like she was holding something back.

"Man," Tiernan tilted her head back to rest against the wall, "I wish I could rewind time and do today over."

"That's another thing we need to discuss. What happened with that reporter?"

"I have no idea. I heard about it in the locker room after the fact." Tiernan had overheard some other golfers talking, and it sounded like the media was saying she'd purposely hurt someone. "There was this guy getting in my face. He grabbed my arm and I guess I shoved him a little, but I don't remember a female reporter."

"The cameraman with channel five let me watch the tape back—"

"What did you have to promise him?"

"I'll never tell. He was pretty cute though." Brit grinned. "Anyway, he didn't get a great angle, but it looked like after you shoved the guy, he backed into this chick and his camera hit her in the face. I talked to medical and they said she refused to get checked out."

"How serious could it be? I mean, I barely touched the guy." Tiernan had already decided the press was blowing the whole situation out of proportion.

"Well, maybe he was playing it up, because on some of the tapes, it looked like he really flew backward. And you can hear a crack when his camera hit her. They were airing it in slow motion on every station tonight."

"Great. So tomorrow I get bombarded with questions about that as well as about Kim."

"Don't worry about the questions. Ignore them."

"How? They're shouting them at me with every step I take."

"We'll let the league handle it. Which reminds me, the brass wants a conference call with you to discuss what they're calling 'recent events.' I convinced them to wait until after this tournament is over, but eventually you need to be available to them."

"Great."

"For now we need to look forward. Tomorrow won't be easy. We're three shots down and Regina isn't going to just roll over."

"She's tough." Tiernan had been up against her before and found her a worthy opponent. Regina was one of a crop of young players, filled with natural talent and zeal for the game that Tiernan hadn't felt in some time. She watched their enthusiasm and remembered with envy the days when every tournament was a new experience. Of course, they would probably give anything to trade places with her and think she was a cry baby for being dissatisfied with her fame and good fortune.

"So let's concentrate on getting your lead back, damn it. I don't want to caddy for the number-two golfer in the league."

Tiernan smiled. "Yeah, thanks for the pep talk."

"Don't stay up too late." Brit patted Tiernan's thigh, then stood and headed for the door.

Tiernan threw her towel on the bench and stepped back on the treadmill. She had a lot more thinking to do before tomorrow.

❖

"Cindy, I'm fine," Elena said for the third time, but her producer didn't listen.

"You could have a concussion." Cindy held the towel-wrapped icepack against the side of Elena's face.

"I don't have a concussion." Elena pulled the towel away.

"Leave it there." Cindy guided Elena's hand back to her head. "What if you lose consciousness?"

"If I haven't already, I don't think I will."

"Well, you might need X-rays or stitches."

Elena pulled the pack away again. "It's just a black eye."

"It's a little more than a black eye." Cindy pressed gently against Elena's cheek. Elena hissed and flinched away.

She sat at the vanity in the dressing area of her hotel room and leaned forward to study herself in her mirror. A half-inch laceration hid just inside her hairline at her temple, and the flesh around her left eye was red and swollen. Elena could already see the discoloration spreading over her cheek and around her eye, up to her brow bone. By tomorrow, she would have trouble hiding the bruise.

"I'm good, Cindy. My hair will cover the cut, and otherwise, I'll just have a hell of a shiner." If Elena had seen a hint of a visible scar, she would have given in and gone to the hospital.

But she didn't want to take a chance that the doctor would tell her she couldn't work tomorrow.

"Take some aspirin or something. You're going to have a headache later."

"Got it, Boss."

"Since you insist you're okay, I'll expect to see you bright and early tomorrow. We're putting you on eighteen again."

"I'll be there."

"Call me if you pass out," Cindy said as she crossed to the door.

"Very funny." Elena turned her head, checking out her cheek from different angles. Since she couldn't do much but apply ice and hope for the best, she stepped away from the mirror. She dimmed the lights, lay down on the bed, and closed her eyes.

"What a day," she muttered.

She replayed the events of the day in her head, beginning with the confrontation in the elevator. Discovering that Tiernan O'Shea was a lesbian had initially surprised her. But the more Elena thought about it, the less shocking the idea became. Tiernan had always fascinated Elena, and she'd assumed her interest was strictly professional. But she now realized that Tiernan possessed an androgynous quality she'd recognized on some level.

More than just her tomboyish appearance and athletic prowess, Tiernan exuded a magnetism that felt familiar to Elena. Familiar. Exhilarating. And scary. Suddenly Tiernan O'Shea was exactly the kind of woman Elena had spent her adult life avoiding. She lived in fear of precisely the same circumstances that Tiernan now faced—being publically outed. The male-dominated world of sportscasting was difficult enough for a woman, without adding roadblocks.

Elena's personal reason for avoiding her sexuality was perhaps even more frightening. She couldn't fathom telling her very traditional Puerto Rican parents that their only daughter was a lesbian. She could imagine the tirade of rapid, unintelligible Spanish that would erupt from her father. And that vein would pop out on his smooth bald head, the one that made her mother worry he was about to have a coronary. Elena preferred to avoid relationships altogether rather than put her family through that. Advancing in her field was far more important to Elena anyway.

And now it looked as if she was making moves in the right direction professionally. Calling the action on the eighteenth hole of a pro women's tournament had been even more exciting than she'd imagined, the highlight of her career so far. But she wouldn't be satisfied until she was a regular announcer on the tour.

However, she didn't aspire to work at the desk like so many of her peers. Though the spots that Bobby and David currently occupied were considered prime assignments, Elena preferred to be out on the course where she could watch the action firsthand. From the booth, the sportscasters could analyze a player's swing on a television monitor in slow motion and freeze the frame.

But Elena got to study the players' expressions as they approached the ball. Did they do so nervously, as if it were the most important shot of the day, or with confidence, knowing they would nail the next shot? Elena felt the excitement of the crowd of spectators as they stirred, then grew silent in tense anticipation. She watched the players sweat and fight to get just a little closer to that lead golfer's score. For her, these things made up the thrilling part of her job.

Chapter Five

T his isn't getting it done, Tiernan," Brit said quietly as they walked down the fairway on the seventh hole.

"I know." Tiernan had begun her day playing merely average golf. She hadn't managed any better than par each of the first six holes. Meanwhile, Regina continued to sink putts for birdie and pulled further away. To make matters worse, the current third-place player was also closing the gap, and Tiernan now had to face not only losing to Regina, but possibly coming in third. "It's just not going my way today."

"That's all you've got? I thought you wanted to win," Brit snapped.

"I do."

"Then let's see it. Get mad. Damn, woman, if you're not going to beat her, at least go down fighting."

Tiernan gritted her teeth and shook her head. She wasn't hitting well, the wind seemed to be against her with every shot, and she felt as if she scrambled with everything she had just to make par. She'd ignored all the inquiries about Kim and the incident with that reporter. But each one seemed to put a tiny dent in her armor. Kim still avoided her calls, though Brit said the media was following her around Orlando so if Tiernan wanted to know what she was doing, she need only pick up a tabloid or listen to any one of the many conversations that seem to suddenly stop when she entered a room.

She needed to put Kim out of her mind until she got back to Orlando and could see her and speak to her in person. She still had no idea what their next step would be, but she'd been with Kim for far too long to simply let things dissolve like this.

❖

Tiernan watched the ball roll along the edge of the hole and hung her head. She'd known for most of the back nine that she had no chance to come back and win. But missing this last putt drove home the point. As Brit bent to pick up Tiernan's ball, Tiernan turned away and headed for the bridge off the island green. She fisted her hands at her side, aggravated with herself for her performance and her inability to effectively handle the events of the past two days. Camera clicks and flashes grated on Tiernan's already tenuous patience, but she held her temper in check.

She continued toward the tent nearby, determined to sign her scorecard and leave without giving the vultures a scrap to feast on. She slipped her sunglasses onto her nose and headed toward the gallery of fans, deciding she preferred dealing with them to the group of media on the right. The crowd parted as if they too were wary after the previous day's incident, but the path they formed led her directly into the cluster of reporters.

The press didn't allow her passage quite so easily, and she was forced to move through them in close quarters. Tiernan still hadn't seen the news coverage of yesterday's accident, so she might not have recognized the female reporter when they came face to face if her injuries weren't so obvious. Tiernan halted, and Brit had to put a hand in the middle of her back to avoid smacking into her.

The woman would be breathtaking, if the bruises hadn't marred the left side of her face. Her skin was smooth and the color of dark honey. Her ebony hair shone beneath the afternoon sun and, fleetingly, Tiernan thought what a shame that it was pulled back so severely. She could imagine it cascading to the woman's shoulders in a shimmering blue-black curtain. When the woman cleared her throat, Tiernan realized she'd been staring.

"Uh, Tiernan O'Shea," Tiernan blurted.

"I know."

Idiot. Of course she knows who you are. The woman's dark suede brown eyes were impossibly hard for such a soft color.

"I'm sorry." Tiernan pulled off her sunglasses, hoping the apology showed in her eyes. "About your…" Feeling inexplicably shy, she touched her own cheek.

"Okay."

"I didn't get your name." This woman wasn't letting Tiernan off the hook. She seemed to be weighing whether or not she wanted to forgive Tiernan enough to even give her name.

"Elena."

Tiernan watched Elena's full lips move and for a moment she couldn't speak. When she finally did, everything seemed to be happening in slow motion. "Elena. Are you okay?"

"I'm fine. Nothing a couple of aspirin and an icepack won't fix."

"I really am sorry."

Elena nodded. Tiernan realized she was still staring at Elena's mouth and forced herself to meet Elena's eyes. They were softer now and filled with an emotion Tiernan didn't know Elena well enough to identify.

A hand clapped down on Tiernan's shoulder and fractured her connection with Elena.

"You need to sign your card." Brit nodded toward the tent nearby where a tournament official waited to escort Tiernan inside.

"Right." Tiernan had no idea how long she'd stood there aware of only Elena, but she was now acutely conscious of how many people had gathered around them watching the exchange. Her stomach fluttered nervously, her limbs felt weak, and for a few minutes, she had completely forgotten the defeat of the past two days. Uncomfortable and uncertain what else she should say, she turned and followed Brit to the tent.

Elena watched in disbelief as Tiernan walked away. The strange exchange had left her nervous and irritated at the same time. For some reason, she'd expected Tiernan to at least know her name. After all, if Elena had given someone a black eye yesterday, she would have taken the time to find out the person's name so, if the opportunity arose, she could apologize.

If Elena had been thinking clearly, she might have injected a bit of attitude into her responses. Instead, she'd been distracted by how close Tiernan was standing. Tiernan had nearly run Elena over before she'd seen her, and by the time she stopped, she was well into Elena's personal space. When she'd removed her sunglasses, Elena had been so caught up in the realization that her eyes looked much bluer up close, that she'd basically stammered through the conversation. After Tiernan walked away, and Elena regained her composure, she kicked herself for how ineptly she'd handled what could have been the perfect opportunity to put Tiernan in her place.

❖

"Kim, pick up the phone," Tiernan instructed through the answering machine at Kim's apartment. Kim kept the place mostly for appearances since she spent most of her time at Tiernan's condo. But she still went there when she was punishing Tiernan for something she'd done—or hadn't done that she should have. "Damn it, I know you're there. Just pick up the phone. You'll have to talk to me eventually. It might as well be now."

A click sounded as the phone was answered and the machine cut off. "What?"

Startled by Kim's abrupt response, Tiernan momentarily floundered. "We need to talk."

"I don't think we have anything to talk about."

"Really?" Tiernan paced the hardwood in her living room. She had stewed about what she would say to Kim during the entire ride home. But despite the three-hour plane trip, she was no closer to sorting out what to do about Kim or her own poor performance in this week's tournament. "You don't have anything to say to me?"

"Like what?"

"An apology."

"Ha. What do I need to apologize for?"

Tiernan could practically see the scowl on Kim's face. She'd always hated to admit she was wrong. "For airing our business on national television."

"If it weren't for you, I wouldn't have been on television in the first place." Obvious resentment made Kim's voice hard. She'd never hidden her dislike for the life she felt Tiernan forced her to live.

"So, now this is my fault for being successful? This whole ordeal hasn't been easy for me either, you know. I got called on the carpet this morning for how my behavior reflects on the tour." She wouldn't soon forget the reaming out the league president had given her via a conference call. He clearly conveyed the message that she should watch her step and carefully consider what kind of press she invited from here forward.

"God, Tiernan, the world doesn't revolve around golf, you know. If you haven't realized that yet, then we don't have anything to talk about."

"You can't pick and choose the parts of my job that you like. You're okay with the travel and the freedom to spend what you want, where you want. None of that could happen if I was a golf pro on some Podunk course in Florida teaching retirees how to swing a club without breaking a hip."

"Why is it always all or nothing with you? All I asked you was to acknowledge our relationship."

"You didn't ask me, you forced me. After your little scene in the elevator, I didn't have a choice."

"And you still couldn't do it, even knowing you were already out in the open."

"Why would I, at that point? You threw me to the wolves." Tiernan allowed her anger to guide her words. "So my options are to face the situation I'm now in either alone or with the person who put me there, a person I obviously can't trust."

"I didn't put you in that situation. You've completely controlled our life together since day one."

"You're really going to blame everything on me?" They'd had this argument before, and Tiernan already knew there would be no winners in the end.

The heavy sigh she heard in response told her that Kim knew it too.

"We'll never change, will we?" Saying the words aloud drove the truth home for Tiernan. This was the end of their relationship.

"No. We won't." Kim's agreement made Tiernan sad but also brought a degree of relief—no more arguing or hurting each other.

"I'm sorry it has to be this way."

After a moment, Kim said, "I've been expecting this for some time."

Tiernan shook her head, in silent denial that Kim couldn't see. "Why didn't you tell me?"

"That's the problem. I shouldn't have had to. We never go out. You never want to do anything that doesn't involve getting ready for your next tournament. I'm bored to tears with our life."

"If you're so damn bored why did you stick around? Nobody made you follow me around the country like a puppy. You could have pursued your own interests." Tiernan echoed Kim's barbed tone.

"You knew I wasn't happy and you weren't concerned enough to really work on things."

Tiernan didn't have an argument for that. She'd known for some time that Kim was dissatisfied with their relationship, and instead of trying to fix the real issues, she continued to slap Band-Aids on the little blowups, trying to pacify Kim with small gestures.

After she hung up with Kim, Tiernan continued to wander around the open space between the living room, dining area, and kitchen. The house had been a reward for herself after her first tour win. She'd been so excited to finally move in, but never had the time to decorate the way she'd envisioned. Eventually, she hired someone to give the place a classy yet comfortable look. The warm hues, plush throw rugs, and expensive vases and paintings scattered around the various rooms accomplished that goal perfectly. But Tiernan still wished she'd had time to personally select each piece. These days, between traveling and training, the only time she spent here was sleeping or trying to grab a couple hours of quiet time before jumping back into her schedule.

Right now, sleep sounded good to Tiernan as she padded through the house to her bedroom, suddenly exhausted. She paused beside her king-sized platform bed and stripped, then pulled on her softest old T-shirt and favorite boxers. Crawling between the sheets, she sighed deeply, wishing she could release her stress as easily as that heavy breath.

Tiernan had never been one for naps, and it was far too early in the evening to turn in for the night. But she couldn't resist the urge to close her eyes for just a moment. Finally, the persistent noise in her head began to quiet. She hadn't slept more than an hour or two for the past two nights because her mind continued to replay the tournament, clicking through the frozen frames of her humiliation like the dreaded images of a friend's vacation slide show that seem to never end.

❖

"Mama, it's not a big deal." Elena wedged the phone against her shoulder and stared at the tabloid in front of her. No matter how many times she'd looked at the picture of herself and Tiernan on the cover, she couldn't shake the surreal feeling. The photo had been taken amid the crowd of reporters while Tiernan tried to apologize. The bruise on Elena's face that makeup had failed to hide stood out vividly enough that Elena suspected the photo had been enhanced to highlight it. Elena had been caught mid-scowl, and even she was surprised at how angry she appeared.

"You have a black eye. Since when is someone beating up my daughter not a big deal," her mother responded in accented English. She and Elena's father had moved to the States while she was pregnant with Elena. She'd learned to speak English quickly, realizing it was the key to success in their new home. But she had insisted that her children be fluent in both languages, that they know both cultures.

"I didn't get beat up. The papers are making the whole thing seem worse than it was. It was an accident. A guy was harassing her, and when she pushed him away he hit me." Elena turned the pages until she found the corresponding article and cringed when she saw the column next to it. The story began with a photo of Tiernan and the woman from the elevator, complete with bathrobe.

"Who is this woman—this golfer who is having all the trouble?"

"She's just one of the players, Ma." Elena leaned back in her desk chair in the small space she'd staked out as an office in her tiny house. The television affixed to the wall over her desk was always tuned to the Golf Channel, but right now the volume was muted.

"I don't like you being associated with people like this, Elena Rosa."

Her mother's use of her middle name took her back to childhood. Appearances were important to her mother, who never wanted her daughter to be treated differently in school. She always told Elena that she would have to be better than some of the other kids just so they would believe she was as good as they were. She drilled into Elena's head the prejudices of the world and how some people would make assumptions about her based on her heritage.

"I'm not associating with her."

"Then why is there a picture of you in the paper? Do you know what others will think?"

Elena suspected she knew exactly what her mother was concerned that these "others" would think. Any hope that her mother hadn't paid close attention to the other article vanished.

"She was apologizing for what happened. And someone snapped a picture."

"Why would you let them put a picture of you like this in the paper?"

"They don't exactly ask your permission before they run their stories."

"I don't understand. I should call someone at this newspaper and complain."

Elena smiled, thinking "newspaper" was a liberal definition for the trash magazine in front of her. She could imagine her mother sitting down to write a letter to the newspaper's editor.

"It will blow over when there's something new to talk about." Nothing Elena could say would ease her mother's mind. She'd never been exposed to this type of publicity before. No one had ever cared enough about what Elena was doing to put it in print, and they still wouldn't if Tiernan O'Shea hadn't been involved. But with her mother, Elena's best chance was to change the subject, so she latched onto a tidbit she recalled about her pregnant cousin.

"Did Lucia get the test results back from her doctor?"

Her ploy worked and her mother launched into a diatribe against modern medicine. Elena listened quietly while she studied the photo of herself and Tiernan O'Shea. The rough paper and smudged, dull colors of the print didn't do justice to the blue of Tiernan's eyes. And the still photograph froze only one of the many emotions Elena had seen pass through them.

When she saw an opening in her mother's monologue, Elena made an excuse about her producer calling on the other line. After promising she would come home for dinner the following weekend, Elena hung up the phone. She picked up the tabloid one more time, then sighed and flipped it facedown on the desk in front of her. She didn't need to look at it again. The image was burned into her memory. Her mother's call had been one of many she'd fielded this morning, and most of the others were from colleagues who found the whole situation humorous. Now, whatever else happened, her professional debut with the tour would forever be a joke.

Chapter Six

D id you enjoy this week?" Cindy sat on Elena's sofa and tucked her feet under her.

"Absolutely." Elena handed Cindy a mug of coffee and set a plate of croissants and jam on the low table in front of her. She settled at the opposite end of the sofa with her own coffee.

Elena and Cindy had become fast friends shortly after Elena started working for ASC. But the previous weekend's tournament was the first time they'd been able to work together on a broadcast. Cindy had been a producer with the network's women's golf division for almost five years.

"Do you want to do it again?" Cindy tucked a strand of long auburn hair behind her ear. Her wavy tresses, clear skin, and bright blue eyes were the reason everyone told her she should be in front of the camera. However, naturally shy but creative, Cindy was more comfortable behind the scenes.

"Really?" Elena's heart lifted. "Yeah, I'd love to. But what about—"

"She can't make it back yet. We'll need someone for a few more weeks or longer. Everyone at the network was impressed with you. Bobby and David, especially, asked for you to return. Can you be in Williamsburg for Kingsmill the day after tomorrow?"

"Sure. Yes, I can." Elena welcomed the opportunity to

extend her time with the pro tour. She had spent the last two days preparing for her next assignment covering a college tournament that weekend. "Can you get someone else to call the Florida State match?" Elena picked up her laptop from the end table next to her, flipped the lid open, and powered it up.

"We can cover that. You just worry about getting to Virginia in time for the first round."

Elena nodded. She was already flipping through her date book, while retrieving her confirmation number from her BlackBerry with the other hand. She hated changing her itinerary at the last minute, but flexibility was a necessary part of her job. So she tried to be as organized as possible to avoid any mishaps. Elena clicked through the Web site she used to make all her travel reservations. "I can switch my flight out tomorrow." She made several quick changes to her search. "No problem. Here's one that will get me there late tomorrow afternoon. I'll run down a hotel room later." Elena noted the new flight information on the calendar in her planner. Later, she would sit down and replace the detailed itinerary she had already prepared for the weekend.

"Good." Cindy touched Elena's arm. "I'm glad you'll be working with us again."

"It was great to be in that atmosphere. Don't get me wrong, I love the enthusiasm of college players. They're full of optimism and they're playing the game for the love of it, not what endorsement contracts they can get. But something about the power and thrill of the professional game gets my adrenaline pumping."

"Well, since you mentioned that, I have another proposition. A space has opened up in the pro-am here in Orlando in two weeks. Do you want to play?"

"Are you kidding? I'd love to." Elena had previously attended the annual tournament as a spectator. The event, which raised money for a local children's cancer-treatment facility, pitted teams made up of one professional golfer and one amateur against each other. The winners took home trophies and prize money. Tiernan O'Shea had been on the winning team for the past four years and always donated her share of the money back to the charity.

"Good. I'll e-mail you the details. There's just one more thing." Cindy looked nervous, but Elena couldn't imagine anything that could dampen her excitement at the chance to play in a tournament with a professional golfer.

"What is it?" She was already anticipating the lessons she might learn by observing a pro that closely.

"Tiernan O'Shea will be your partner."

Elena stared at Cindy while the metaphorical wet blanket saturated her enthusiasm.

"I've already talked to the tournament officials and her agent, and they promised she would behave. They think pairing the two of you would be good press, like you're burying the hatchet."

"What? It's not as if we have some big feud. The whole situation was blown out of proportion. When will everyone let it go?"

"When they find a hotter story. I agree, they're hanging onto this a little too hard. But in the meantime, it's exposure for the network."

Elena hated for the network to use her life to get their name out there, but since they signed her paychecks she didn't have much leverage to change that fact. If she'd wanted to be involved in gossip journalism, she would have gone to work for *The Informer* instead of a legitimate network. "No press is bad press?"

Cindy raised her hands, palms up. "That's true. Luckily, it's not a side of the entertainment business we have to deal with too often."

The fact that the sports network didn't usually get embroiled in tabloid-type news stories only made Elena feel more awkward about her role in the latest coverage. Then again, why should she feel guilty? After all, she hadn't hit herself in the face with a camera. Now as a result of an unfortunate accident, she was trying to lay low until the publicity died down. But it sounded like the network wanted to put her out front and center, and, by agreeing to pair her with Tiernan, the league was going along with it.

"I need to let them know something soon, so they can find someone else to play if you're not available."

"Available? Of course, I'm available." She'd be crazy to turn this opportunity down. But was playing in the tournament really worth spending eighteen holes with a very moody Tiernan O'Shea? And thinking about what her mother would say about the idea made her shiver.

"Then why do I get the feeling you're still not sure?"

"Do they even care if I can actually play? Would they be asking me if it weren't for the incident over the weekend?"

"Sweetie, you wouldn't even be a blip on the radar if it weren't for that." Cindy's tone was unapologetic. "That's why you should do this. You may not get another opportunity like it."

Basically, Cindy was advising her to enjoy her fifteen minutes, because the press would soon move on. Though Elena looked forward to that day, she had to admit that the idea of playing in a pro-am was exciting.

"Okay. I'll do it." Elena made a note on the calendar still open in front of her.

"Good. And I'll have someone send you the schedule, assignments, rosters, and such for the next few tournaments. At this point, we're playing things by ear, but you can plan on working with us at least until the pro-am and possibly after."

❖

"Promise you'll hear me out before you say no," Brit called as she crossed the gym, weaving closely around the various weight equipment.

"What is it?" Tiernan didn't pause in her reps and continued to silently count the pull-downs as the bar touched her chest then rose again. Tiernan had converted the large room in her house into a gym after she tired of working out at the neighborhood facility down the street. She'd spent her entire athletic life under a microscope and sometimes she just needed privacy. She cherished the times when she could work out here or swim laps in the pool out back in solitude.

"Promise." Brit paused as if she actually expected Tiernan to make the vow.

"Brit, tell me."

"Okay, I'm getting some calls. But the most interesting one was from the Equal Rights Initiative."

"Why did they contact you?" Tiernan was familiar with the organization, which dedicated itself to gay rights and lately had focused on the very current issue of same-sex marriage.

Brit sat on the bench next to Tiernan and hooked her ankles around the padded bar, but made no attempt to lift the stack of weights. "The director's sister works with my sister, and she gave him my number. They want you to speak at a fundraiser they have coming up."

"Absolutely not."

"Hey, I said hear me out."

"I'm not doing it." Despite the vehemence of her reaction, Tiernan released the bar in a controlled motion and stood up. She crossed to the other side of the room and, after taking only a second to check the weights, picked up a barbell.

"Why not?"

"I refuse to be some dyke poster girl." Tiernan curled the bar up, straining with the effort of lifting the weight that was almost too heavy for her. Normally, she kept her weights lighter, striving for flexibility and lean muscle, but today she was working off stress and aggravation.

"And how is that different from what you're doing with Spin?"

"They're my sponsor."

"Oh, so the difference is, they're paying you to pimp their clothing, whereas the ERI is asking you to volunteer to help their cause."

"Don't do that."

"What?"

"You know what. Don't make me sound greedy. This is my job."

"Wearing their visors and polos is your job? Because I thought you were a golfer. I wasn't aware that the clothing you put on actually affected your game."

"Damn it, Brit." Tiernan's already short temper flared.

"Think about this invitation seriously before you say no. You're already out—"

"Not by my own choosing," Tiernan grumbled.

"You didn't have any say in how it happened and that makes you angry. I get it. But how you handle things from here *is* your choice. You have a chance to do some good and take back control of this situation." Tiernan opened her mouth, but Brit wasn't done yet. "Consider it. You can be a role model for a whole new population of young people, reaching further than just golf."

Tiernan paused and looked at Brit. Maybe she couldn't feel okay with the way things went down yet, but she could appear as if she was okay. She nodded. "I'll think about it."

❖

Four days later, Tiernan still hadn't decided if she would accept the offer from the ERI, despite Brit's continued insistence that it was a good idea. She had to admit, the opportunity to make something positive out of the situation appealed to her. But she was still sulking over her very public embarrassment.

And she hadn't had time to thoroughly sort out her thoughts about the recent changes in her life. She'd been too busy fighting to stay in the running at Kingsmill. Now Tiernan stood in a crowd of her peers trying to look gracious as the trophy was presented to Regina Paine. Regina had played four good rounds and ended at sixteen under par, so Tiernan couldn't fault her for the win. Tiernan's own sixteenth-place finish stung more than a little. But she clapped politely as Regina smiled and held up her prize.

As the ceremony concluded, Tiernan turned away and a cluster of reporters immediately confronted her. She veered to her right but was blocked by another group of media clamoring for Regina's attention.

"Tiernan, how do you feel about your performance this week?"

The first question she heard struck her as so absurd that she laughed aloud. When she looked up, she spotted Elena lurking near the back of the pack surrounding her.

She bit back a sarcastic response and summoned the public persona she'd been donning since she was a college standout at Duke. "Obviously, I'm not pleased by the way I finished this weekend." When she met Elena's eyes the amusement shining in them led her to believe Elena caught the sarcasm she couldn't keep out of her voice. "I missed several opportunities for birdie and that eagle putt on fifteen."

"What will you do to prepare for next weekend?"

"Train. We plan to work hard this week in the gym and on the course. Brit and I will isolate some areas I fell short in this weekend and concentrate on not making the same mistakes again."

"Will you try to see Kim?"

Tiernan rolled her eyes and decided against decorum. "Come on, guys. Isn't that old news yet? I think you've invaded our privacy enough."

A bark of laughter came from a man Tiernan recognized as a representative from a popular sports magazine. "We didn't invade anything. You both put your business out there with your show in the elevator."

The sting in her chest in response to his barb surprised Tiernan. She nodded slowly and ground her teeth against the comeback that clawed against the back of the throat. Without another word she forced her way through the crowd and only distantly heard the mumbled comments of the press as she passed.

Elena watched Tiernan walk away for the third time in just over a week. What had she gotten herself into? Granted, her colleague's comment was out of line, and Tiernan hadn't necessarily provoked it. Maybe Elena's desire to avoid Tiernan was unfair to her, but Elena didn't welcome the scrutiny she would no doubt face by being paired with Tiernan in the pro-am.

"Who would've predicted the mess she's got herself into?"

Elena turned at the smugly spoken words from behind her. Dakota Mayer's eyes followed Tiernan's trek into the clubhouse with a disgusting leer on his face. Elena ignored his comment but he kept talking.

"This is why I don't like working in women's sports. Too much drama. Why can't women athletes learn to keep their personal problems to themselves and just play the game?"

"Oh, and the men are so good at that?" Elena knew there was no point in engaging him, but she couldn't let his comment go.

"Yeah. Men know that business is business and all that other bullshit shouldn't interfere."

"Really? I can think of at least two baseball players in hot water for doping, a football star facing charges for soliciting a prostitute, and another for beating his cheerleader girlfriend. Then there's a certain male golfer we all know who can't even step on the course without his obligatory morning cocktails."

"Okay. But those are just a few examples."

Elena wanted to point out that he was giving only one example to support his position, but decided she didn't care that much about winning this particular argument.

"A lesbian," Dakota muttered. "I always knew there was something a little off about her."

She just stared at him.

"What?" He puffed his chest out defensively. "I can spot 'em, you know."

"Whatever." He probably based his assumption on the fact that he'd asked Tiernan out and she hadn't given him the time of day. Of course, Elena figured any woman he hit on that had half a brain would quickly be able to see past what she supposed was considered an attractive face and decent body. In her experience, Dakota Mayer had very little actual substance.

Tiernan O'Shea, on the other hand—there was definitely some mystery about her. When Tiernan had pulled off her sunglasses in irritation, Elena noticed a depth of emotion in her stormy blue eyes that intrigued her. In a couple of weeks, Elena would be close enough to find out more. Surprisingly, although that thought frightened her, it also excited her.

CHAPTER SEVEN

Tiernan pulled a nondescript baseball cap lower over her face and slipped on a cheap pair of sunglasses. She laughed at herself as she stepped out of the car into the Florida sun. In the three weeks since Palm Springs, she'd been reduced to avoiding the media and drawing as little attention to herself as possible. She'd never been a social butterfly, preferring to spend her time on the course or in the gym. Now, when she did venture out, she dressed to blend in, choosing bland clothing devoid of her sponsor's logo. Her silver Lexus coupe didn't stand out among the luxury vehicles of Orlando's well-to-do, and the media had finally stopped camping out outside of her house. They hadn't completely lost interest, but now they reported her struggles on the links between more current gossip about a certain Hollywood couple, whose marriage was apparently on the rocks, and their drug-addicted teenage son.

A knot formed in her stomach as she looked at the three-story brick building in front of her. Fighting the urge to get back in the car and drive away, she forced herself across the parking lot to the front door. She'd been summoned to the office of her agent, Wally Rubenstein, by his secretary. When Tiernan commented that she didn't sound her chipper self, the woman tersely repeated the appointment time, then hung up with no further small talk.

The three tournaments since Palm Springs had been a disaster. After a disappointing finish at Kingsmill, she'd gone home and subjected herself to her most grueling weekend of training ever. Even Brit had asked her to slow down. But Tiernan ran for miles, as if she could outdistance the dread churning in her gut. She lifted weights until her arms ached so badly she feared she couldn't lift a club, then forced herself onto the driving range to hit ball after ball to the point of exhaustion. And when she was certain she'd drained herself of every remnant of energy, she retreated to the sauna in an attempt to sweat invisible toxins out of her body.

But despite her self-imposed punishment, she didn't play any better in the next two tournaments. Her best finish was eleventh, only because everyone else seemed to play as badly as she did that weekend.

So she entered Wally's office certain he planned to give her a stern lecture. As she walked into the reception area, the secretary waved her inside Wally's private space without a word, and Tiernan's apprehension ratcheted up. Usually, she had to endure at least ten minutes of pictures and stories about the woman's genius grandson before she was allowed an audience with Wally.

She knocked lightly on the faux-wood door and heard Wally invite her in. He had been her agent since she first qualified for the tour, and his office hadn't changed. Sports memorabilia still covered every available surface, the only additions those of new clients as they achieved success. A display case on the far wall held a ball from every tournament Tiernan had played in since signing with him.

Tiernan stepped close to his polished mahogany desk and spilled three new golf balls from her hand onto the padded blotter in front of him. He gazed at her through the thick lenses of his wire-rimmed glasses, then at the display case, and finally down at the balls in front of him as if he didn't even want to put them in with the others.

"Sit down, Tiernan." He rubbed a hand over sparse strands of oily black hair that were stuck to his balding head in a ridiculous comb-over.

"What's going on, Wally?" Tiernan remained standing behind the chair across from him.

When he sighed heavily, his jowls jiggled and Tiernan tried not to stare.

"The folks over at Spin are raising some red flags."

Tiernan wrapped her hands around the back of the chair and squeezed until her knuckles paled. Her sponsors were nervous. That was never a good thing. If Spin dropped her and word got out, she'd have trouble getting someone else to put up the same kind of money. They'd been good to her, and now wasn't the time to be shopping new endorsements. She'd be lucky to be shooting commercials for orthopedic-shoe inserts.

"It's because I'm a lesbian, isn't it?"

"No."

"It's always like this. This is why I kept it a secret for so long—"

"Tiernan—"

"Those damn bigoted mother—"

"Tiernan!" His voice finally sunk in and Tiernan stopped. "It's not because you're a lesbian. It's because you're losing."

"I'm…" Tiernan stared at him and hated the pity she saw in his rheumy eyes.

"You haven't had a good showing in any of your last three tournaments. What's going on with you?"

"What's the big deal? Other golfers have good weeks and bad weeks. Nobody gets upset if they don't win every one."

"You've got a seven-figure endorsement deal. Do you know how rare that is in women's golf?"

"Of course, I do." The contract Spin had offered had thrilled her, and she prided herself on her management of that money. Instead of blowing her windfall on exotic cars and fancy meals, she'd hired an accountant and invested most of it. She didn't plan on being broke when she eventually retired from golf.

"Well, then, it's simple math. They pay you to wear their clothes. If you don't stay at the front of the pack, you don't get as much air time from the television stations, and their clothes don't get seen. Is this really so unexpected?"

"Yes." Tiernan raised her voice. "Yes, damn it. What happened to loyalty?"

"Spin is your sponsor, not your family. You won't find any loyalty there. Come on, Tiernan, you haven't even broken the top ten since Palm Springs."

"So what? They're pulling my deal? Don't we have a contract?" Tiernan snarled at the reminder of the weekend when all this drama started.

"You know contracts can be broken. They'll cite some damn morals clause that you didn't even know was in there and say that the bad press you're getting lately could damage their reputation."

"Sure. Unless *I* was the one who wanted out, then the contract is ironclad, right?"

"Companies write these things to protect themselves. We got you the best deal we could at the time, but—"

"Yeah, well, right now the deal sucks, Wally." Tiernan raised her voice, then, defeated, she sank into the chair. "It just sucks."

"I know, kiddo. So far, they're just making threats. I'll keep talking to them and see if I can work it out. But you need to stop whining and start winning, or we won't have any leverage."

Tiernan flinched. He'd never pulled any punches with her, and he obviously wasn't starting now. "Geez, do you think I'm not trying?"

"Are you?" Before she could answer, he threw up his hands. "Now hold on. All I'm saying is something is different. I watched last week's tournament and those girls didn't even have to work very hard to beat you. You're not the same balls-out kid I signed eight years ago. You gotta figure out how to get the fire back in you."

"If you have any ideas, I'm all ears."

"Get with that miracle-working caddy of yours and figure it out." He flipped several pages on his calendar. "You have the pro-am starting Saturday. Do something press-worthy there and it'll take some of the heat off."

"Seriously? My chance at redemption is the *pro-am*? What if I get stuck with a dud of a partner? In top form, I might have been able to carry someone else, but with the way I'm playing lately—"

"I got a call from the tournament organizers and they're putting you with Elena Pilar."

"The reporter?" Tiernan knew exactly who she was.

"Yes. I think they're just looking for some good press. People will tune in to see the two of you together."

A vision of them together—intertwined—flashed unexpectedly in Tiernan's head. Elena was tall and lean, with an athletic build that Tiernan imagined would fit perfectly next to her own body. She blinked quickly to dispel the image.

"Is she any good?" Clearly, Tiernan's first concern should be doing well in the tournament, which meant she needed Elena to be more than eye candy.

"Rumor is she played in college. I guess you'll find out in three days."

❖

"Beer?" Brit held up a sweating bottle as Tiernan sat across the table from her.

Though tempted, Tiernan shook her head. Just then the waitress came over and Tiernan ordered bottled water. She glanced at the menu quickly before choosing the most low-calorie selection she could find. Brit ordered crab legs and fried clams.

"We're in a seafood place and you're ordering salad." Brit glanced at the waitress. "Don't you have a rule against that?"

The waitress smiled and left to put in their order.

"They never know how to respond when you do that," Tiernan said. Brit knew Tiernan controlled her diet carefully during the season and delighted in trying to tempt her to indulge.

And Tiernan enjoyed firing back. "It wouldn't hurt you to eat a few salads, you know."

"Ha. This is all muscle." Brit patted her belly proudly. Brit had the kind of metabolism that made other women hate her.

Their food came and Tiernan picked up her fork, but the reminder of the event ahead quelled her appetite. "I met with Wally today."

Brit paused in the process of deconstructing crab legs and drenching them in drawn butter. "Yeah? What about?"

"Spin is nervous about my recent—uh—lack of performance on the course."

"What? They're getting ahead of themselves, aren't they?"

"I think so."

"We're going to turn things around," Brit said confidently, before she resumed her assault on the crab legs.

"You haven't heard the best part."

"Hmm?" A mouthful of food muffled Brit's response.

"I'm playing with Elena Pilar in the pro-am."

"Wow." Brit jerked her head up and visibly swallowed. "Publicity stunt?"

Tiernan nodded. "That's the general consensus."

"It's a good move really. Your audience is already changing since you came out—"

"Got pushed out is more like it."

"Either way. You're out. And I'm noticing a lot more lesbians in your gallery crowds."

"Really?" Tiernan hadn't paid much attention to her spectators lately.

"Oh, yeah. I mean it's not like a Melissa Etheridge concert or anything, but more than before. So pairing you with a hot woman will make the lesbians happy."

Tiernan let Elena's face float into her head. Her sultry eyes and thick dark hair definitely could evoke a fantasy or two. "She *is* pretty hot."

"Hell, yeah. The woman is smokin'. Think she can play?"

"I sure as hell hope so. I gotta show Spin something before they decide they can do better with Regina Paine or somebody."

"You're really worried about this?"

"Jesus, my luck hasn't been that good lately, Brit."

"I thought you didn't believe in luck."

"Well, after this week, I might just become a convert. Maybe I need a good-luck charm."

"Or a superstition." Brit's eyes lit up with humor. "Like, when you win again you won't change your socks?"

Tiernan grinned. "Nothing disgusting like that. I'm single again, you know. I'll never find someone new if I smell like a sweaty sock."

"Ah, the libido returns. Things are looking up already."

"I don't know about that. I need to be focusing on golf, not women."

"There's time for both, my friend." Brit raised her bottle in mock salute. "And you better learn that fact quickly because I bet you start getting offers from all kinds of available lesbians."

"I doubt it."

"Please, an openly gay female golfer. You'll have women falling all over you."

Tiernan cringed at the phrase "openly gay," then reminded herself she might as well get used to it. Despite things not going the way she would have preferred, the sooner she became accustomed to her new identity, the better off she would be. Brit sounded as if she was encouraging Tiernan to be a player, but Tiernan knew better. Brit was old-fashioned at heart. Despite what she might say, Brit was holding out for her Prince Charming.

"Speaking of which, I've had some more interesting offers from gay and lesbian organizations all over the country. I think you should consider some of them."

"Why?" Tiernan shoved her half-eaten salad to the side and planted her elbows on the table.

"Because some positive publicity couldn't hurt."

"Why don't you let Wally worry about the PR side of my

career? Your responsibility is my golf game and that's not going very great right now."

"My responsibility?"

"Oh, you know what I mean. I couldn't do this without you." Though she realized Brit already knew how much she appreciated her, Tiernan suspected she needed to hear it sometimes.

CHAPTER EIGHT

E lena pulled into a parking spot in the player lot at the Orlando Pro-Am, but she didn't turn off the engine. After taking only a moment to enjoy being in the player lot, she forced her mind onto the task ahead. She flipped down the visor and checked her makeup in the mirror. As she stepped from the car, she plucked her BlackBerry from its designated pocket, then scrolled through the day's schedule for about the tenth time that morning. She'd already committed each block of time to memory, down to the minute, but glancing once more at the itinerary she'd created helped her breathe easier.

She opened the trunk of her '67 Mustang and lifted out her club bag and a small duffle. The Mustang's faded Arcadian Blue exterior stood out among the sleek and shiny luxury cars in the lot. Elena scanned the vehicles, wondering which was Tiernan's. A row away, she spotted Regina Paine exiting a white late-model Mercedes. She shouldered her bag and strode past Elena without a glance.

Elena slung her arm through the strap on her own bag and headed for the clubhouse. The butterfly wings beating against the inside of her ribs didn't slow a bit as she entered the locker room a few minutes later. She fought the urge to look at her BlackBerry again, but in the end she relented, clicked through the screens quickly, and the tension in her chest eased a bit. Then she took a deep breath, dropped her duffle on a bench, and sat down next to it. Feeling out of her element, she sent up a silent prayer that at least she wouldn't embarrass herself. She'd been on the range and playing local courses as much as she could since she found out she would have this opportunity.

The tournament organizers had a tent set up on the well-manicured lawn at the side of the clubhouse. As she approached she spotted Tiernan lounging against the corner post of the tent and her nervousness multiplied again. Elena couldn't look at Tiernan anymore without thinking, *this woman is a lesbian,* and today she looked damn good. Her blond strands were highlighted with pale wheat shades and stylishly tousled. Light khaki shorts contrasted with the golden length of her legs. When she recognized Elena she straightened and stretched, making her lean body appear even more elongated.

Elena had only seen Tiernan in passing since their meeting in Palm Springs. Other than that moment at Kingsmill, Tiernan had avoided eye contact the few times they'd passed each other on the course. Elena might have taken it personally if Tiernan hadn't been the same way with everyone. She sulked around the courses, making no time for the press and, more surprisingly, little time for her fans as well. But since she and Tiernan were about to spend the better part of two days together, Elena vowed that she, at least, would be friendly. If their time as partners was miserable, it wouldn't be Elena's fault.

"Good morning," Elena called out, determined to be as cordial as possible. "Looks like we're going to be partners."

"Yep. I've already signed us in." The corner of Tiernan's lips twitched as if she wanted to smile but the impulse didn't sufficiently communicate with her mouth. The sunglasses shading her eyes prevented Elena from searching them for the emotion behind Tiernan's expression.

When Elena set down her bag, several balls fell out of a pocket she'd left unzipped. While she chased two that escaped down the sidewalk, Tiernan picked up the one that rolled up against her shoe.

Tiernan tossed the ball up in the air, then caught it, trying to appear more relaxed than she felt. "Have you played much?" Despite the more non-competitive nature of this tournament, Tiernan needed to look as good as possible on the course. Spin Golf probably wouldn't pull her endorsement just yet, but it couldn't hurt her relationship with them if she and Elena had a good score at the end of the two-day tournament.

"I played on my college team, but since then it's been strictly recreational."

"Handicap?"

Elena gave Tiernan a curious look. "About ten. But aren't we just here to have a good time? It's for charity, after all."

Tiernan nodded absently. She didn't need to let Elena know how much she had riding on this tournament. A ten handicap was good for an amateur. If Tiernan could get her game together, they might have a shot, especially since some of the other celebrities viewed this weekend as a chance to get face time in front of a camera.

"Should we warm up?"

"Sure. It's over here." Tiernan picked up Elena's bag and walked around the tent. She glanced over her shoulder several times, then stopped when Elena caught her.

They arrived at the driving range where pyramids of golf balls were stacked near each practice area. Brit waited next to Tiernan's bag. "Hey, Brit." Tiernan greeted her with a slap on the shoulder. As Brit slid her eyes quickly over Elena, curiosity was evident in them. Tiernan tried to convey a warning in her own gaze. "Elena, this is my caddy, Brit Dailey. Brit, Elena Pilar."

"Right, I'm familiar with your work," Brit said with a smile.

"As am I with yours." Elena glanced at Tiernan as if to indicate that Brit was responsible for her success.

Brit laughed. "Nice. Welcome. I look forward to seeing you play today. Is your caddy here yet?"

Elena looked over her shoulder toward the parking lot. "Not yet."

"Well, there's still time yet. I'm about to go grab some water. You guys want anything?"

"Water, please," Tiernan said.

Elena shook her head, and Brit nodded and walked away.

Tiernan pulled a wedge from her bag and, holding it along her shoulders, twisted at the waist. She'd stretched thoroughly earlier, so she didn't need to loosen up, but the motion was habitual. She continued through some light stretching and covertly watched as Elena pulled a BlackBerry out of her pocket, then shoved it back in as if irritated at the device.

"Expecting a call?"

"What? Not really. Well, my brother—my caddy—is apparently running late and hasn't let me know."

"I'm sorry. Do you need me to see if I can find someone else for you?" Tiernan took out her own phone, confident she could get someone to come and help them out.

"No. He'll make it. Maybe at the last minute, but he'll be here."

Tiernan chuckled. "Sounds like you're used to that."

"Yes. I'm the punctual one in the family."

"Punctual? Or habitually early?"

Elena took an easy practice swing, hoping she didn't look as awkward as she felt. Nervousness made her motions stiff. "Early. Almost always. Are you usually late?"

Tiernan shrugged. "I tend to believe that I'll get there when I get there. Unless it's a tee time, of course. Then I like to be very early. I take more warm-up time than anyone out here, I think."

"Well, you wouldn't be where you are if you weren't serious about your game."

"Where I am isn't exactly an admirable place to be right

now." She was playing the worst golf she had in nearly a decade and was far too close to losing her endorsement deal.

"No, I don't envy your personal situation. But professionally—"

"Professionally, I'm not in much better shape." Tiernan only realized how telling her words were when it was too late. The interest in Elena's eyes as they spoke felt genuine, and Tiernan had forgotten Elena was a reporter. The troubles she'd been having lately were well documented, but, though they were common knowledge, she didn't want the fact that she was stressing about them broadcast to the public.

Fortunately, she didn't have to explain why she suddenly clammed up because Brit walked toward them with a Hispanic man trailing her. Right away, Tiernan could tell he was the missing brother. He shared Elena's slender build, smooth-milk-chocolate eyes, and the slight indentation at the tip of the chin.

"Look who I found. He was wandering around the clubhouse asking everyone if they knew you. Luckily I came along when I did." She handed Tiernan a bottle of water.

"Yeah, she rescued me."

"Tiernan, this is my brother, Vincent."

Elena watched them shake hands and noted how similar they were. Not in appearance, because Vincent's dark hair and eyes were the opposite of Tiernan's. But they both wore their emotions on their faces, and as they greeted each other their expressions were open and friendly.

"Are you a golfer, Vincent?" Tiernan asked as she rolled a ball in the grass with the end of her club.

"No. Not at all. Elena is the athlete. I'm the geek."

"What do you do?" Tiernan glanced at Elena, dropping her eyes down, then letting them trace back up her body. She smiled slowly, and the sensual pull of her lips made Elena's stomach flip. The reaction itself wasn't surprising, because Tiernan was an attractive woman. But Elena missed the jolt of panic that usually followed such flashes of awareness. She didn't experience the sudden fear that someone would find out, would see her desire for a woman.

"I'm in IT. I manage the network for an international shipping company," Vincent said.

"Sounds interesting." Tiernan set up quickly behind the ball and struck it smoothly, then immediately rolled another ball over and sent that one sailing after the first.

She continued to do so, all the while carrying on a conversation with Vincent about his family. Vincent spoke fondly of his wife and two children, but Elena was intent on Tiernan's face, which was a mixture of interest in their exchange and concentration on the balls she was hitting. When she glanced over and saw that Brit had noticed her watching Tiernan, Elena lowered her head and took her place in the area beside Tiernan and started warming up as well.

Elena almost managed to work through half the clubs in her bag before Brit warned them they had less than ten minutes left. They both took out their drivers and began to hit long balls. Tiernan's out-distanced Elena's by at least forty yards, but Elena was still quite pleased with how straight she kept her shots. She saw Tiernan sneaking peeks over her shoulder and waited to hear her opinion, but Tiernan didn't offer one. So instead she tried to guess what Tiernan might think. Objectively, she was a slightly better-than-average golfer, and despite her nervousness, she was pleased with the shots she put out there. But trying to figure out what Tiernan was thinking derailed her concentration and she hooked two in a row. So she forced Tiernan out of her mind and focused on swinging correctly and contacting the ball solidly.

Chapter Nine

All of the butterflies Elena had been able to banish on the driving range returned full force a half hour later as they walked from the clubhouse toward the first tee and the beginning of their round. She was about to play in a tournament with the best female golfer in the game today, some would say the best women's golf had ever seen. That was a daunting thought and difficult to reconcile with the friendly woman who had just chatted easily with both Elena and her brother.

But if she needed a reminder of who Tiernan was, she got it as they passed a group of reporters who began hurling questions at them. Most were directed at Tiernan, those Elena expected, but she was surprised to hear her name peppered among the onslaught.

Tiernan adjusted her sunglasses on her nose and ignored them. "Like dogs with a bone," she muttered when they'd passed the crowd. "I'll be so glad when someone else screws up. Maybe then, I'll be old news."

Uncomfortably aware that she was part of the fraternity Tiernan blasted, Elena didn't respond.

"I mean, can you imagine having no more purpose in your career than to harass someone to the point that they can't live their life?" Tiernan looked at Elena and her expression changed, as if she'd just realized what she had said and to whom.

"You're right. Chasing a little ball around in the grass is a much nobler purpose."

"I'm sorry. I just—lately they've—you've—"

"It's okay." Elena didn't know how else to accept the incomplete apology.

"I guess neither of us is changing the world with our livelihoods." Despite the obviously forced lightheartedness of her tone, Tiernan's words were laced with self-reflection.

"Do you want to change the world?" Elena asked.

Tiernan shrugged. "I've never given it much thought. It seems like I've been on this path all my life. Maybe I don't have a greater purpose than playing golf."

"I don't know. We're here, raising money for charity, aren't we?"

"That we are." Tiernan nodded.

"So, how is everything else going?"

"Everything else?"

"Um, Ms. Donovan?" Elena hadn't kept up with the tabloid coverage, but she hadn't heard anything about Tiernan and Kim being seen together.

"It's not—going, that is. Kim and I are through. It's for the best, really." Tiernan sounded sure. She didn't seem to be just putting on a brave front.

"How are your friends and family dealing with finding out about you?"

"I have only a couple of close friends and they already knew."

"And your family?" Elena couldn't imagine choosing to tell her family about her own orientation, let alone having the media foist it on them.

"My mother and I aren't close. No siblings."

"My mother would freak out if I told her I'm gay." Elena spoke without thinking and saw the surprise on Tiernan's face before she covered it up. She glanced quickly behind her and found her brother engrossed in conversation with Brit. Her choice of words didn't make it entirely clear if she really was gay or giving a hypothetical, so she plowed on before Tiernan could question her. "Did you at least get to tell her before she read it in the papers?"

Tiernan shrugged. "Not really. But it doesn't matter."

"Did she and Kim ever meet?"

"Are you interviewing me?" Tiernan's tone suddenly turned icy.

"No," Elena said. She didn't intend to relay this conversation to anyone else. "Completely off the record. I was just...making conversation. But your ex is probably not what you want to talk about, is it?"

The suspicion melted from Tiernan's eyes. "No. Not really. I imagine my life story is pretty well-known. Let's talk about you."

Tiernan's bio *was* well-known, and Elena had surfed the Net to refresh her memory after she found out about the pro-am. Tiernan's mother and father had divorced shortly after the scandal of his infidelity broke in the media. Then reports about Tiernan's mother became scarcer.

"My life's not all that interesting."

"Tell me how you got into broadcasting."

"I kind of fell into it. In college I got a job at the campus radio station and we covered all the university sporting events. The other students wanted to be the DJ, but I was content doing sports."

"Have you worked professionally in any other sports, or strictly golf?"

"I started at a local station here in Orlando and manned the sports desk. But after I got the job with ASC, I mostly covered college golf. Until a few weeks ago, that is, when one of the regular broadcasters got sick."

"That explains why I don't remember seeing you before."

"The day of our...incident with that other reporter's camera was my first time working a professional event."

Tiernan winced. "Sorry about that. I guess I really made a good first impression."

"That wasn't my first impression."

"No?"

Elena grinned, hoping to soften the blow. "I was in the elevator with you and Kim that morning."

"What? Really?"

Elena nodded.

Tiernan's eyebrows furrowed. "You'd think I'd be able to remember every detail of that morning perfectly. But honestly, I don't recall anyone else being in the car."

"I'm not surprised. You were kind of wrapped up in your conversation."

"Yeah, I guess so."

They stopped talking as they got within earshot of a crowd of spectators gathered around the first tee. Tiernan led Elena through a narrow corridor made by tournament security, and once inside the roped-off area they put some distance between themselves and the onlookers. Brit and Vincent waited for them behind the tee area with their respective bags.

"I can't believe how nervous I am," Elena said quietly.

"Why?"

Elena smiled. Of course, Tiernan didn't understand what standing on the first tee at such a highly publicized tournament felt like for her. "I've never had this many people watch me play golf before. Did you ever get nervous? Or were you always so cool under pressure?"

Tiernan seemed to be considering the question, and Elena wondered how many years she had to think back to recall feeling nervous on the tee.

"My first year on the tour, I thought I'd throw up before every tournament."

"Yeah, that's a fairly good description of how I feel right now."

Tiernan pulled her driver from her bag and palmed a ball. "Are you ready?"

Elena chuckled. "No. You go first."

Tiernan stepped onto the tee box. But when her name was announced, she barely acknowledged the round of applause from the spectators. She glanced down the wide fairway before lowering her head and addressing the ball. Her swing was fluid and appeared effortless, a sweeping arc of the clubhead back, then more quickly forward as her body uncoiled and drove the ball. She ended in a textbook position with her hips facing down the fairway and the club cocked over her left shoulder.

"Your turn," Tiernan said as she rejoined Elena.

"Just like that, huh? You make it look easy enough."

Tiernan shrugged. "I guess when you've had a club in your hand from the age of three, it's like breathing. It's hard to imagine not playing every day."

"You've played every day since you were three years old?"

"Pretty much. Ever since I can remember. This was my dad's dream for me, too."

The announcer introduced Elena, so she turned her attention to the tee box. "I suppose it's time." The casual conversation with Tiernan had eased some of her nerves. But she'd seen Tiernan's expression change when she mentioned her father and was glad they wouldn't venture too far down that path right now. She remembered reading that Tiernan's father passed away while she was in college and didn't want painful memories to affect Tiernan's game today.

Elena took her driver from Vincent and teed up her ball, but when she glanced at the crowd waiting expectantly, her nerves returned full force. Her palms started sweating and her muscles tensed. She took a quick practice swing, but the motion felt awkward and stilted. Deciding she'd better hit the ball before she clammed up too much more, Elena took her place and set her club behind the ball. In the middle of her backswing, she knew she was in trouble but she couldn't stop. Her shot went off the toe of the club and began its flight, sailing too far to the right immediately.

Elena mumbled a curse and turned away as her ball disappeared into the tree line along the right side of the fairway. What a great way to start her first round. The clicking of shutters around her reminded her to hide her frustration. She took a calming breath and slowly slid her club back in her bag, all the while avoiding Tiernan's eyes. She didn't want Tiernan to think she would have to carry them through the next two days.

Expecting Vincent to follow, she headed down the fairway, ignoring the curious looks of everyone she passed. No doubt they were all asking themselves who she was and how she'd gotten in the tournament, and feeling sorry for Tiernan for having a lame partner.

While Elena was still kicking herself for succumbing to nerves, Tiernan fell into step next to her. She walked so close their shoulders nearly touched.

"Don't beat yourself up, kid. It's best ball," Tiernan said.

"Sorry." Elena couldn't read Tiernan's expression. The reminder that the rules of the tournament dictated they would play the best of each of their shots didn't make Elena feel better. She hoped she could come up with some good ones and they wouldn't spend the whole day playing Tiernan's ball.

"It'll be a long two days if you let the first shot follow you."

Elena nodded, confused. Tiernan was an emotional golfer and Elena had seen her silently chastise herself for missing a putt or hooking a drive, so her easy acceptance of Elena's botched attempt was surprising.

Tiernan slowed as they reached her ball and let Elena go in front of her. "Why don't you hit this next one first." She hoped Elena's second shot would be good enough to ease her mind of her first error. Her own gut had clenched as Elena shanked her first, but she was determined not to let that misgiving blow the rest of their round. If need be, she would just have to step up her game to make up for Elena's amateur play.

Obviously still uncertain about his role, Vincent was basically shadowing Brit. When Brit set down Tiernan's bag he did the same. With a tilt of her head, Elena beckoned him forward and he rushed toward her, leaving the bag standing where he'd dropped it.

"Bring the bag," Elena whispered.

"Sorry," he replied, clearly flustered.

"Never mind. It's okay." Elena stepped back to her bag and pulled out a club.

"I've never done this before and I'm nervous."

"I know. It's fine." When Elena laid her hand on his shoulder, Vincent looked at her with adoration. Tiernan searched Elena's face for the same affection and, while she found it in Elena's slight smile, the emotion was more veiled.

Vincent resumed his place at Brit's side and Elena settled into her stance beside her ball. Elena's chest rose as she drew in a deep breath, then took her shot. Her swing appeared effortless as her ball flew into the air and dropped onto the green.

"Very nice," Tiernan said as she stepped close to Elena again.

"Thank you."

When Elena moved out of the way, Tiernan nearly duplicated Elena's ball flight, placing hers within a foot of Elena's on the green.

"Show-off," Elena teased.

Tiernan grinned widely in reply.

"Could you do that again?"

"Probably eight times out of ten." Tiernan exaggerated slightly, but she *was* very accurate from inside a hundred and fifty yards.

"I have to admit, I'm a little jealous." Elena handed her club back to Vincent.

Tiernan shrugged. "My dad used to set up drills like that for me, and I kept going until I got twenty in a row within a foot of the flag."

Elena could imagine Tiernan, as a child, practicing late into the night, stopping only when dusk turned to dark. She'd witnessed Tiernan's passion for the game, or was it for winning? Her enthusiasm had certainly dimmed since she'd begun to struggle. "So he saw your natural talent and nurtured it?"

"Something like that. He traveled a lot, but when he was home he took me to the course with him. He gave me a club he cut down to my size to keep me quiet so I wouldn't disturb him during his training sessions." Tiernan smiled wistfully. "I had barely learned to walk. But he carried some old balls in his bag for me to play with, and I couldn't have been happier."

When they arrived at the green, Vincent and Brit handed them their putters. Tiernan circled the hole, staying clear of both their balls. Etiquette dictated that she not step on the path between a ball and the hole.

"Yours is the better putt," Elena said. Both balls were about five feet from the pin, but Elena's was on the side of a slight rise in the green.

"I think you're right."

Elena scooped up her ball as Tiernan readied herself to putt. Since they were playing best ball, if Tiernan missed, Elena would get a chance to try the same shot. But with a short, light stroke, Tiernan put the ball in the cup.

"Birdies are always good," Brit said as she took Tiernan's putter, then patted her shoulder.

They'd finished the hole at one under par, a good start to their round. Elena breathed deeply and some of her nerves dissipated. But the tournament had just begun, and she was determined to do her best to help Tiernan win.

❖

Six holes later, Tiernan stared down the longest fairway on the course. The wind was in her face, and she doubted anyone was reaching this par five in two today. If they got to the green in three they could make par or maybe squeeze out another birdie. They'd shot one under for five of the seven holes so far, and Tiernan figured they must be near the front of the pack.

"You should go for the green here," Brit said, holding out Tiernan's five wood.

"I don't know." Tiernan hesitated. She needed to carry a small creek down by the green. Both sides of the fairway were lined with thick trees, and if she got in them, she'd waste a stroke punching it back out.

"I do." Brit paused until Tiernan met her eyes. "You've got this one." When Tiernan nodded, she smiled. "And if you don't, Elena hits after you, and we can have her lay it up on this side of the creek."

"Shouldn't we be playing conservative?"

Brit laughed. "Are you feeling okay? I usually have to talk you into playing safe."

"I need a win here, Brit."

"Hey, don't get too focused on that and let it mess up your game. We just need to do what we do, and I promise it will fall into place."

"Yeah?"

"Don't second-guess yourself. It's not who you are. Besides, you and Elena are a good pairing and I'm confident the two of you can pull it off."

Tiernan glanced over at Elena, who stood a few feet away conferring with her brother. They *had* worked well together so far. Elena solicited Tiernan and Brit's advice, then did her best to follow it. And as they made their way through each hole, she kept up a steady conversation. Despite Elena's initial nervousness, judging by the beaming smile that constantly graced her lips, she enjoyed playing.

At times, Tiernan, ever conscious that Elena was a member of the media, got nervous that she might say something that would end up on the news or in print, but most of the time it just seemed as if she was talking to a new friend.

Friendly, however, didn't completely describe how Tiernan felt when she looked at Elena. Several times, she'd caught herself watching the way Elena's body moved when she swung, the tightening of her thigh muscles beneath the hem of her khaki shorts, and the way the fabric of her polo clung to her breasts as she finished a swing with her club high over her left shoulder and her chest out. Looking at Elena made Tiernan feel slightly breathless, but the one time Brit noticed, Tiernan had covered by saying she was only thirsty. She proceeded to chug half of a bottle of water in an attempt to quench the rising flame of desire.

Elena and Vincent continued to look down the fairway, and Tiernan wondered if they were having a conversation similar to hers with Brit. She could barely hear their murmured voices, but it was clear they were speaking Spanish. Perhaps it was just because the language was foreign to Tiernan, but she found Elena's low, almost husky tone and the rapidly spoken phrases incredibly sexy. She smiled when she realized she was beginning to find everything about Elena Pilar attractive.

"Hit this green." Brit pressed the five wood into Tiernan's hand.

Tiernan laid the clubhead down behind the ball and went through her pre-shot routine, flexing her knees and looking along her left shoulder at her target, a red flag waving in the distance. She lowered her head and focused for a second on her ball before drawing her club back. After years of playing, Tiernan could sense the quality of her contact as soon as she struck the ball. She could almost feel the tiny vibrations of a perfectly struck ball travel up the club and into her arms. She smiled before she even finished her follow-through and watched it fly toward the flag, dead-on, then drop off in time to bounce just short, hop up on the putting surface, and roll to a stop about twelve feet from the hole.

"Very nice." Brit gave Tiernan a high five and picked up her bag.

Elena and Vincent both congratulated Tiernan on her shot, when they joined them. She grinned and told Elena, "Put one up there next to it."

"I'd like to, but I don't know if I can be that accurate from this far away."

"You've got the distance for it." Tiernan was a fairly long hitter and she had watched Elena's shots land just thirty to forty yards behind hers on several holes so far. "Do you have a three wood in that bag?"

"Yes."

"I'm already on. What do you have to lose? Just rip it."

"Yeah." Elena pulled her three wood and strode over to her ball like a woman on a mission. She set up over the ball with confidence and swung smoothly.

She definitely had the distance, but she wasn't quite as on-target as Tiernan. Her ball landed on the slope leading to the right side of the green, but it took a bad bounce to the right and rolled off the hill.

Elena turned toward Tiernan with a beaming smile and shrugged. "I guess I don't quite have that shot."

"Yeah, maybe we need to work on that one." Tiernan grinned back.

Chapter Ten

Tiernan stared at the huge leaderboard posted just off the eighteenth green. She and Elena were actually in first place. Elena had just sunk a birdie putt and they had finished at eight under for the round, three shots in front of the second-place pairing.

"Are you okay, pal?" Brit touched Tiernan's arm.

"We're winning. I mean, I just wanted to play some good golf, but we've actually got a chance to take it all." Even when Tiernan heard the team behind them approaching the green, she didn't move. She'd been struggling for weeks and she felt so good to be winning again.

"Things are turning around. I don't want to say I told you so, but—"

"But you told me so," Tiernan said. "I never thought I could be so happy to be leading a charity pro-am."

"Come on. Let's go sign that scorecard."

Tiernan followed Brit to the nearby tent, where she and Elena went inside to turn in the record of their score for the day. Tiernan watched Elena as she looked over the card before she signed. She seemed to be trying to play it cool, but Tiernan could tell she was a little in awe of her surroundings. As a member of the media, she would never have been allowed inside this tent. Tiernan smiled as Elena scrawled her name on the card, then handed it over to the league's official scorekeeper.

"This was fun." Elena's smile made her eyes dance.

Fun? Tiernan couldn't remember the last time she'd applied that label to golf. She did enjoy the game, but many years had passed since she'd played a non-competitive round. She even executed her practice rounds as if an entire tournament rode on her score. *You practice as you will play.* Tiernan heard her father's voice and felt the lick of guilt against her conscience when she realized she *did* have fun playing with Elena.

"We're in great shape heading into tomorrow's round." Tiernan glanced at the leaderboard through the gap in the tent opening.

"You sound surprised."

"I am. A little." The burden on Tiernan's shoulders felt a hundred pounds lighter. "This isn't an easy course, and it's a strong field."

"You're a daunting competitor, you know. Don't count out your intimidation factor."

"Intimidating? Not lately."

"Maybe not. But everyone knew you'd get it back in order. And you did today."

Tiernan shrugged.

"What's going on? I've never gotten the impression you became negative about your game even when you weren't dominating a tournament." Elena exited the tent and Tiernan followed.

The question was unexpected and Tiernan paused to think before she answered. "It's been a rough few weeks."

"But weren't you due? At least professionally."

"How so?"

They walked, shoulders nearly touching, along the cart path toward the parking lot where Brit and Vincent were already loading their clubs into their cars.

"You've had the Midas touch for quite some time. Can you really complain about a few weeks of trouble?"

"I would have thought not. But apparently Spin is getting nervous."

"So?"

"So if they drop me, I lose a ton of money in endorsements."

"And? Is your career over without their money? That seems a bit greedy. Thousands of young women would give anything to play professionally, thinking nothing about lucrative contracts."

"That's a nice sentiment, but in reality, pro golf is a business."

"Business should be mutually beneficial. If Spin won't stand by you, should you really stress about letting them go?"

That sounded simple enough. Was it really that easy? Could she just tell Wally that Spin would either back her or they wouldn't? If word of that ultimatum got around, would she be able to get another endorsement deal? She was still a championship golfer. Certainly someone would want her name attached to their product.

This kind of thinking was precisely what Elena was referring to, pimping out her name to line someone else's pockets. Tiernan had come to believe that endorsements were a necessary part of pro golf, but were they really? She didn't need the money. She could win enough in tournament play to leave her more than comfortable. So was it just a pride thing? Bragging rights—that an internationally famous sports-apparel company wanted to put their name on her.

"Would you like to have dinner with me tonight?" Tiernan blurted as they drew closer to their cars. Even though she would see Elena tomorrow, she wasn't ready to part from her yet.

"I'm sorry. I have plans."

"Another time then."

Elena hesitated. She wasn't sure what was behind Tiernan's invitation and didn't know how to respond. If she intended the evening to be a date, Elena couldn't agree. But if Tiernan simply wanted to have a friendly dinner, Elena didn't want to make a big deal of her refusal. "Yeah, maybe."

Tiernan laughed.

"What?"

"I've been shot down enough to know when I'm getting the brush-off."

Elena had a difficult time believing that Tiernan had been rejected very often. She had an expressive face and an aw-shucks demeanor that was simply charming. But her reaction gave Elena a clue about what she expected from "dinner."

"I don't think it's a good idea," Elena said.

"It could be a great idea."

"I guess that's a chance I'll have to take."

Tiernan laughed. "Okay. I'll see you tomorrow then."

"Sure thing. We've got a tournament to win." Elena glanced at the next row of parked cars where Vincent waited next to her car. "I'm over here."

Tiernan watched Elena walk away and replayed their conversation in her head. She had no idea what made her ask Elena out, but she hadn't expected that answer. Considering the vibe she'd gotten from Elena and her one cryptic comment about her sexuality, Tiernan thought Elena would take her up on her invitation.

"You're enjoying this." Brit's words abruptly interrupted Tiernan's musings.

"What?" Startled, Tiernan's tone was harsher than she intended. Had Brit overheard their conversation?

"The tournament."

"Of course, I am. We're winning."

"That's not what I'm talking about. It's been a while since I've seen you smile like that, especially during a round of golf."

"It's a charity tournament, Brit. It's supposed to be fun."

"You've still got a lot riding on it."

"You said we would be okay," Tiernan shot back.

Brit raised her palms in a defensive gesture. "Don't get

worked up. I think it's a good thing." Brit looked at Elena, who was still walking to her car. "She's a pretty good golfer."

"Yeah. She is." Tiernan followed Brit's eyes. She was certain she was studying Elena a bit more closely than Brit, noticing the way her ponytail swung gently from side to side as she moved. When her gaze drifted downward she watched shapely hips and a firm backside mirror the motion. "We have a chance this weekend, don't we?"

"I think so. When you're on, nobody can touch you. And you may not quite be back there, but she's picking up the slack nicely."

Yes, she was.

❖

Elena was still thinking about Tiernan's invitation two hours later as she walked through the front door of her parents' house. No matter where she went or what she accomplished, whenever she stepped through that door she remembered that as a Puerto Rican daughter, everything she did reflected on her family. The fact that she was unmarried and childless disappointed her parents, specifically her mother, who viewed it as her own failure in much the same way that her father basked in Vincent's success and machismo.

She hadn't lied about having plans. She couldn't have begged off dinner with her family to go out with Tiernan, not without some explanation, and she definitely wasn't bringing Tiernan to her parents' house.

The savory aroma of asopao de pollo filled her senses as soon as she entered the house and her stomach growled, reminding her that she hadn't eaten anything since a granola bar at breakfast. She'd been too nervous. After posting a good score today she could breathe a bit easier, and her appetite had returned full force.

"Mama," she called as she passed through the entryway,

though the greeting was merely a formality. Her mother would be in the kitchen. The hallway leading to the back of the house was lined with family photos, and it seemed new ones were added every time Elena visited. Only now, instead of Vincent and Elena featuring prominently, Elena's niece and nephew held that honor.

In the kitchen, Elena's mother lifted the lid from a large pan on the stove, and steam wafted out. She stirred the simmering chicken-and-rice stew, then sampled it.

"Dinner smells wonderful. What can I do to help?"

"You can set the table. But say hello to your father first. He's on the porch."

"Of course. How's he doing today?"

"Very well."

Elena's father had begun to show signs of the beginning of Alzheimer's earlier that year. Though he still had more good days than bad, he was doing more than just forgetting where he put the keys and becoming confused more frequently. Elena hated watching the once-strong head of their family deteriorate. Most days he was aware enough to know what he was missing, and on those days his recent uncharacteristic behavior hurt his pride. He'd been raised to believe he was solely responsible for providing for his family, but since he couldn't work, Elena's mother had taken a job cleaning houses. He was too proud to take money from either Elena or Vincent, but Elena snuck several hundred dollars a week to her mother when he wasn't watching.

She found him on the covered porch that ran along the length of the house, rocking slowly in his favorite chair and gazing out over the small backyard. The faint creak of the porch floor and the lilting song of a nearby bird were the only sounds. Elena pushed open the screen door and he turned toward her.

"Hola, Papa." She stepped outside and hugged her father.

"Vincent says you played well."

"I did okay. We're leading, but that's mostly due to Tiernan."

Elena sat in the rocking chair next to him and pushed off gently with her toes.

"Tiernan?"

"She's a golfer, Papa. I told you they had assigned me to play with a professional. She's very good." Since her mother was concerned about Elena's name being attached to Tiernan's, the odds were good that she hadn't shown him any of the articles in the paper about Tiernan in the last few weeks. She would have wanted to spare him the worry she harbored about Elena's reputation.

Vincent rounded the corner of the house in time to hear Elena's words. "You were carrying her." He sat on the top step and propped himself against the railing.

Elena laughed. "Hardly."

"She's not as great as everyone says. Although it is a shame she's the way she is, because she's pretty good-looking."

"What way?" Elena's father asked.

"She's not Catholic," Elena answered quickly, giving her brother a stern look. For her father, that was only slightly less of a sin than being gay. "But I'm not going to her church. We're just playing golf."

"Has she invited you to her church?" Elena's father asked.

Vincent snickered.

"No. She hasn't." Elena didn't tell him that she'd been "converted" many years ago. But since she hadn't dated anyone since college, technically she guessed she could be considered lapsed. When she was in college and living in the dorm, she had little trouble distancing herself from real life and her family's judgment. But since she'd returned to the old neighborhood and bought a house just down the street from them, she was too worried about them finding out to take a chance with anyone. "Anyway, after tomorrow, I won't be spending any more time with her."

The feeling of disappointment that shadowed that statement

surprised her. But Elena stuffed the response down. Despite how much she looked forward to tomorrow—to seeing Tiernan and to playing again—she needed to remember that after the tournament was done, things would return to normal.

❖

"I asked her to have dinner with me and she shot me down," Tiernan said as she dragged a tortilla chip through melted cheese. After Elena rejected her, Tiernan had talked Brit into coming out for Mexican food. She hadn't been watching her diet as closely these past few weeks, and tonight she put off her vow to be more responsible for another night in favor of spicy burritos and mariachi music.

"Who?" Brit sipped her margarita. Tiernan had opted for water with lemon, drawing the line at consuming alcohol the night before a round.

"Elena."

Brit laughed.

"What?"

"Are you serious?"

"Well, I was."

"Honey, you are forbidden fruit for all but the most out lesbians right now."

"What are you talking about?"

"You're getting too much press. *If* Elena is a lesbian, and I haven't heard even a whisper that she is, she's definitely not out and probably won't risk being connected to you."

"She already is. We're playing together."

"Precisely. Which is why she won't want to spend any more time with you than necessary." Brit took another drink, offered her glass to Tiernan, then set it back down when Tiernan shook her head.

"I think she might be a lesbian."

"What makes you say that?"

"Just a feeling."

"Either way. You should probably avoid women for now anyway. You need to be focusing on golf. You'll have time for relationships later."

"Damn, I didn't want to be single again. I hate dating."

"Yeah, all of those hot, young lesbians throwing themselves at you. You've got it rough."

"You know it's not like that. I don't have enough time to spend with someone to even figure out if we have a connection. Perhaps, like you said, I should avoid dating altogether." Tiernan grinned as a new idea occurred to her. "But in the meantime, maybe I could practice flirting again."

"You think so?"

"Well, you know, you practice how you play." Tiernan borrowed her father's words and wondered, not for the first time, if he would have accepted her sexuality.

Brit laughed. "Yeah, that's true. And you're nothing if not dedicated. So you really plan to use this theory as an excuse to flirt with Elena?"

"Why not? She's interesting, smart, and gorgeous. It can't hurt to test the waters."

"Well, then—" Brit raised her glass—"here's to testing the water."

Tiernan clinked her own glass against the rim of Brit's. As much as she enjoyed the thought of getting to know Elena on a more intimate level, Tiernan did need to keep her priorities in order. And tomorrow, her first concern was maintaining their lead and winning the tournament.

CHAPTER ELEVEN

Tiernan strode into the locker room late Sunday morning full of confidence. She'd slept well for the first time in weeks and awakened feeling rested and positive about the day.

Elena sat on a bench in the center of the room, pulling on her shoes. Her outfit was perfectly matched and utterly feminine. Her pink polo brought out the same color in her pastel plaid skirt. When she looked up, Tiernan recognized the Spin Golf Apparel logo on her pink cap.

"Nice hat." Tiernan dropped her bag on the next bench, unzipped it, and took out shorts, a polo, and a visor. Since they had one of the last tee times of the day, Wally had booked her an interview on a local television station's morning show. From there, she'd come directly to the golf course and still wore a button-down and khakis.

"You like it? It was delivered to my house this morning. At first I thought you'd sent it. But then I saw the note." Elena pulled her knee up to her chest and reached around to tie her shoe.

"Note?"

"Wally Rubenstein sent it on behalf of Spin. He said they wanted me to have it and hoped it would bring me luck in today's round."

"It's all about publicity," Tiernan muttered, then to Elena she said, "You don't have to wear it."

"I know. But I like the color. And I already had an outfit to match. Besides, I didn't want to offend your biggest sponsor."

"Don't worry about that. You ready to win this thing today?"

"Absolutely."

"Good. We're going to kill it." Tiernan tugged her blouse free and unbuttoned it.

Elena nodded, wondering what inspired such an obvious change in Tiernan. She stood up at the precise moment that Tiernan turned toward her. Through the open front of her shirt, Elena glimpsed the plane of Tiernan's smooth stomach and quickly averted her eyes. Intent on getting ready to play, Tiernan didn't notice Elena's distraction and slid her shirt off her shoulders. Beneath it, a pale pink, lacy bra encased Tiernan's small breasts. Elena once again tore her eyes away when she noticed the bumps of Tiernan's nipples inside the delicate cups. Tiernan's torso was pale in contrast to the deep tan of her arms and neck, a combination Elena was sure could be attributed to many hours spent on the course.

"We need to play clean today. We can take a few chances, especially if we stay well in the lead, but for the most part, I just want to finish strong." Tiernan continued to talk strategy as if she didn't notice that she didn't have Elena's full attention—at least not on what she was saying.

When Tiernan pulled a sports bra from her bag and reached for the clasp between her breasts, Elena spun away quickly.

"I—I'll meet you on the range." She hurried through the door without waiting for a response.

Elena made it halfway across the lobby before she released the breath she'd sucked in when she realized Tiernan intended to strip bare. She didn't slow her stride until she exited the back door of the clubhouse into the morning sun. But the heat that spread over her at the sight of Tiernan's stomach hadn't yet receded, and the desire to feel skin under her hands still lingered.

She spotted Vincent and Brit waiting on the driving range, and reality chased away her distracting thoughts. For the next several hours, she should stay focused on playing the best golf she could. She'd agreed to play in the tournament because she thought it would be a great experience, but now that they had a chance to win, she was even more excited and committed.

❖

Standing at the side of the third tee box, Tiernan watched Elena bend and tee up her ball. She jerked her eyes away and completely turned around before anyone could catch her ogling Elena's backside. But, geez, did she have to wear that damn plaid skirt that pulled snugly across her ass when she bent over? As Tiernan did a one-eighty she caught Brit's eye and saw a small smile play over her lips. Tiernan sent her a warning look, but Brit just grinned in response. Tiernan turned back around to watch Elena's shot.

Elena glanced up as she set up for her drive and Tiernan saw her expression change when she realized Tiernan was watching her. Elena's attention lingered on Tiernan's face, a fleeting expression that just touched her features, but to Tiernan it felt as if she were looking deeper. The moment was over quickly when Elena closed her eyes briefly, severing the connection. Tiernan looked away and then heard, rather than saw, Elena's shot. She could tell by the metallic ping of the driver that Elena had made good contact. A second later, cheers from the spectators around them confirmed this.

Tiernan was still distracted as she climbed the small hill to the raised area designated for teeing off. She didn't look at Elena, but she felt her presence and caught the spicy scent of her perfume as they passed each other. The strip of fairway that stretched out in front of her was long and straight, and Tiernan had been hitting this kind of shot for more than half her life. So she didn't hesitate to tee up her ball and rip it down the center.

"Nice shot. That was a long drive," Elena said as Tiernan stepped down from the tee box.

"Thanks." Tiernan had been praised for her golf game for most of her life, and the drive hadn't even been particularly impressive. But still Elena's compliment made Tiernan feel good.

"What's your longest drive?" Elena asked as she fell into step next to Tiernan and they walked toward their balls.

"I don't have a clue."

Behind them, Brit and Vincent toted their bags and, over the shuffle and mumble of fans trying to keep up with the group, Tiernan could just hear their clubs clicking together rhythmically.

"You don't know."

"Ask one of them." Tiernan waved her hand at the gallery trailing them. "I'm sure they know my stats better than I do." Elena didn't reply, and when Tiernan looked over at her, Elena's brow furrowed. "What?"

"If I were in your place, I would know my stats inside and out."

Tiernan smiled. "I hardly know you and that doesn't surprise me."

"What do you mean?"

"You would have them programmed into that PDA of yours. And you would probably have them on a computer somewhere, charted and graphed, right?"

"Maybe."

Tiernan laughed at Elena's apparent reluctance to admit this characteristic.

"What's wrong with being informed—with knowing the trends in your game?" From the edge in her voice, Tiernan guessed this wasn't the first time Elena had defended this particular trait of hers.

"Nothing. I think it's cute. I should probably be more up on that stuff. But Brit does such a good job of tracking my game and telling me the things I need to know. The rest of that stuff is just numbers, and I'm afraid to let them limit me."

"How could more information limit you?"

"When I get up there, I don't want to be thinking about stats. If I'm thinking that my longest drive is two hundred eighty yards or whatever, I might not feel like I can do any more than that. But if I let instinct and training work in my favor, maybe I can hit it just a little farther."

"I'm the opposite. I need to see things in black and white, usually several times, before I feel comfortable."

"The secret to golf isn't driving distance anyway. It's accuracy. You can drive the ball three-quarters of the way down the fairway, but if you screw up that second shot and don't get on the green in two, you're no better off than a shorter driver who takes three to get on."

"That's a good point. And you've probably been driving far enough to be in contention on the pro tour since you were, what, eight years old?" As if to punctuate her point, Elena bent and swept her ball off the grass before they continued on to Tiernan's, forty yards away.

Tiernan laughed. "Well, probably not that early. But if I'd had my way, I would have gone pro at sixteen."

"Why didn't you?"

"My mother insisted that I graduate college. She's not a big fan of golf as a career." Tiernan's mother blamed golf for the demise of her marriage. Tiernan knew she always hoped her constant harping about college and other career paths would somehow outweigh Tiernan's desire to play golf.

"So you went to Duke."

"Yep. It was a good school. Far enough away from the folks, but less than a day's drive if I got homesick."

"You joined the tour before finishing your degree, didn't you?" Elena had obviously been studying Tiernan's bio.

"Yes." Tiernan didn't want to explain her reason for leaving Duke. She'd never make it through a conversation about losing her father before he got a chance to see her go pro without crying.

"Have you thought about going back?"

"I haven't had the time. But I would someday if I felt I needed to."

"Just the satisfaction of getting a degree wouldn't be reason enough?"

"Why do I need a diploma when I have everything I could want without one?" As soon as she spoke, Tiernan realized how harsh her tone was. She sighed. "I'm sorry, it's a touchy subject. My motivation for being in school died with my father. That's really all I can say about that right now." During her darkest days, following her father's funeral, Tiernan and her mother had argued violently about her future. Their relationship had been unsalvageable since then, and talking about it would bring back far too many emotions for Tiernan. She refused to lose that much control in front of a golf course full of people and television crews. "Do I need to ask you to keep that between you and me?"

"Of course not."

"Thank you. It's not as if that part of my life isn't well documented, but I'd prefer not to dredge it up right now."

"As with anything we've talked about these last two days, it's totally off the record."

Tiernan nodded, then over her shoulder, she asked Brit, "Looks like about a hundred and thirty left, right?"

"Yes." Brit handed Tiernan a club.

Tiernan took a moment to study her shot. Then, with an easy swing, she pitched her ball onto the green, but she didn't get enough roll and it stopped about fifteen feet short of the hole.

"See. It's no good if you don't deliver on the second shot. Stick it close for us," she said as she passed Elena. She had a makeable putt and they could still finish with a birdie, so she wasn't nervous about Elena's shot.

Elena nodded and settled into her stance. She stood over the ball for a few seconds longer than she had on previous shots, looking at the flag then back at her ball and at the flag again. She hit the ball well, a fluid motion, letting the club do the work for her. The ball bounced just off the green, then skipped on, ran right toward the hole, and finally dropped in.

Elena whooped and raised her arms in the air, then looked around her and dropped them as if she'd just remembered where she was.

"Sorry." Despite the apology, her expression showed no remorse, only joy.

"Why? It was a great shot. You *should* enjoy it."

"Sure. But I could do it a bit more graciously. Like a subtle fist pump."

"Hmm, yeah, the fist pump has gained popularity. Everybody wants to be Tiger Woods. I say do something different."

"I'll have to think about it a bit." Elena smiled. "You don't have a signature, do you?"

"Not really. I just go with what I'm feeling at the time. I've never been very good at holding back my emotions."

As Tiernan said the words, she realized how true they were, both professionally and personally. Her sexuality was the only thing she'd ever hidden about her life, and now, she didn't need to do that. Perhaps that was the blessing in the most recent events. Would she ever think that being out of the closet outweighed the negative impact of these past few weeks?

CHAPTER TWELVE

Elena took her scorecard from her back pocket, but when she looked at it, the numbers didn't change. She and Tiernan had consistently made par, interspersed with a few birdies. But one of the other pairings was making a move, and their lead had been cut to only one stroke. Elena began to put the card back in her pocket, then pulled it out to stare at it again.

"Stop looking at that thing," Brit said from beside her.

"I like to know where we stand."

"You won't find what you need to know on that card, anyway."

"So, where will I find it?"

"Over there." Brit pointed across the green where Tiernan crouched, studying their putt. "Eighteenth green. Long putt. This is where champions are made."

Tiernan was the picture of concentration, completely still as she leaned against her putter shaft and her eyes repeatedly tracked the path between their ball and the hole. Elena tucked the card back in her pocket and crossed the green. They had this putt for par and a win, but if they missed, they would need the next for a tie and then proceed to a playoff against the other pairing. The ball rested just inside the fringe on the opposite side of the green from the hole. Elena began to mentally prepare for a playoff.

"You can make this," Tiernan said when Elena stopped next to her left shoulder.

"Me?" Elena had assumed Tiernan was analyzing the shot so closely because she planned to attempt it first.

Tiernan nodded.

"That's a twenty-footer. Why don't you just go ahead and put it in if it's so easy."

"Because I want to watch yours first. Come down here." Tiernan tugged on the hem of Elena's skirt until Elena knelt beside her. "You read putts for a living."

"Sure. Other people's, not my own." Elena hoped Tiernan couldn't hear the slight tremor in her voice. She attributed it to nerves, not to the electricity radiating from the spot on her thigh where Tiernan's knuckles had brushed a moment ago.

"Okay. So tell me. If I'm the one about to take this shot, how would you describe this line to the viewers?"

"Really?" Elena turned her head slightly and Tiernan's breath feathered across her cheek. Tiernan waited with an expectant expression. Elena looked back at the ball in front of her and then at the hole. She traced the expanse of green between the two and could see the track the ball would take as clearly as if a chalk line were drawn on the surface. Playing along, she assumed a professional on-air tone. "Okay. She's got a lengthy putt that's going to fall off left about three-quarters of the way to the hole. It's a ways uphill, so she'll really have to smack it to get it up there."

"Good." Tiernan straightened, and when Elena stood, she felt Tiernan lightly touch her waist before stepping away. "Now hit it just like that. I'm sorry, *smack it* just like that."

Elena nodded and stepped up to the ball. She took one last look to check the line and aimed about eight inches to the right of the hole. Her putt was firm, with what she hoped was enough steam to get it up the rise that began in the middle of the green.

"Looks close," Brit said quietly from somewhere behind her.

Tiernan whispered, "It's off an inch to the left." The ball

tracked almost the exact path Elena had predicted it would take. But she hadn't put enough on it and it was breaking harder to the left than they had thought. The ball rolled across the endless expanse of green, then stopped just short and at the left edge of the hole.

"Damn," Elena muttered.

"It was a good attempt." Tiernan wrapped her hands around her putter and lifted it, testing its weight. She had changed putters last year and until recently had been pleased with the results.

"I came that close and I missed it."

"Don't beat yourself up. That's a good lag from that far back."

"Ha. You would expect yourself to make that."

"Probably." Though a number of golfers on the tour would be satisfied to two-putt from twenty feet, Tiernan wasn't one of them. "At least before my run of bad luck these past few weeks. But since I've seen your line, I'll be even angrier if I don't make it."

Having watched Elena just miss, Tiernan didn't need more than a few seconds to set up for her putt. Now aware of what the ball would do, she adjusted for the increase in break. She took a firm stroke, and as soon as she got it started she knew it was on course. As the ball dropped in, Tiernan looked up at Elena and gave a controlled fist pump, then smiled wide. Her losing streak was over.

Brit embraced her hard. "Great job, buddy." Grinning, she took Tiernan's putter.

Tiernan lifted her ball from the hole and threw it into the crowd that filled the bleachers around the eighteenth green.

Elena rushed across the green and, for a moment, Tiernan thought she might throw herself into Tiernan's arms. She was both bracing for and eagerly anticipating the impact when Elena drew up short and visibly collected herself.

"Well done." Elena stuck out her hand.

Tiernan considered pulling her in for a hug, but the hesitance in Elena's eyes dissuaded her. So, instead, she clasped Elena's hand in both of hers and squeezed.

"Are you sure I can't take you to dinner to thank you for playing with me this week?" Even though she'd already been shot down once, Tiernan couldn't help asking again. She didn't want her time with Elena to end.

"I think I made myself clear last time you asked. Calling it a celebratory dinner doesn't change my mind." Despite her casual tone, Elena glanced nervously at her brother. If she was a lesbian, she apparently wasn't out to her family.

"Okay. Well, I guess I'll see you around the courses."

"Yes, maybe." Elena slipped her hand free of Tiernan's.

"Maybe?"

"I've been filling in for a colleague and don't know how long that will continue."

"I thought maybe you were planning a career move, possibly thinking about trying your hand at pro golf." Tiernan veiled her disappointment with Elena's rejection in light humor.

"Absolutely not. This was fun. But I prefer the less stressful weekend rounds at the local courses."

"Me too, sometimes."

"Oh, please, I've watched you play plenty of times. You thrive on the excitement and the pressure."

"Yeah, I guess I do. Now let's go submit our scorecard and make this official." Tiernan led Elena toward the tent, and as the crowd parted she paused to grant a few autographs. One fan asked Elena to sign alongside Tiernan's signature, and Elena tried to graciously refuse, but in the end she gave in. However, Tiernan could tell she was uncomfortable with the attention.

"Hey, thanks for coming. I just couldn't make myself go into the office today," Cindy called from a chaise lounge when

Elena walked onto the patio behind Cindy's sprawling ranch home.

Since, during the season, they were on the job through almost every weekend, it wasn't uncommon for them to take a day for themselves during the week. Elena hadn't wanted to work today either, especially since she'd hit the snooze button on her alarm a half dozen times that morning. After her win in yesterday's tournament, Elena's family had taken her out for dinner, an evening that spilled into the late night and eventually involved her entire extended family. They had plied her with margaritas until she gave in to their urging to provide a blow by blow of what it was like to play in a tournament, and with the number-one woman golfer, no less.

"Sit, please. I don't want to crane my neck while talking to you," Cindy said, gesturing at the chaise next to her.

Elena complied. She stretched back on the lounge and the sun warmed her skin quickly, until soon she was thinking about jumping into the sparkling pool before them.

"I saw highlights from the tournament on the local station last night. You played great."

"Thanks. But I was partnered with Tiernan O'Shea. I couldn't lose."

"Funny. Because she's been losing plenty lately. Maybe you brought her good luck." Cindy picked up a glass filled with some sort of frozen concoction. "Can I get you a drink?"

"No, I'm fine."

"Listen, we'd like you to do some interviews about what the tournament was like."

"No." Elena had already refused more requests than she could count, and she would continue to do so. Aside from her desire to keep her privacy, she also didn't want to share her time with Tiernan with anyone else, and she wasn't foolish enough to think she could do an interview that was only about the golf. The questions would eventually lead to Tiernan's personal life.

"You won't reconsider?"

"You knew how I felt about this up front. I haven't changed my mind."

Cindy nodded. "Okay. As your friend I admire your resolve. As your producer, I'm frustrated. We're missing some opportunities here."

"I'm sorry," Elena said, only to be polite. She wasn't sorry in the least. "The collegiate championships are coming up. Will I be going back in time to cover them?"

"Actually, the spot you've been filling has opened up permanently and the network would like you to stay on the pro-tour team."

"Really?" Elena was shocked that Cindy would make such an offer after she'd just refused to cooperate with the network's wishes.

"Don't act so surprised. You've done a good job. And you've gotten them some great publicity."

"I hope that's not why they're offering it to me, because I plan to stay out of the spotlight from now on. I'm eager for things to get back to normal."

Cindy reached into a briefcase beside her chair and pulled out a folder. "Here's the remainder of the season's schedule. You can count on being on the team through the end of this year. Go ahead and make your travel plans. I know you like as much notice as possible."

"Thank you." Elena took the folder. She set it on the table beside her, resisting the urge to pull out her BlackBerry and check her schedule for the coming weeks.

"Welcome aboard. Officially."

Elena smiled, wondering if a fist pump would be inappropriate. She'd made it, at least for this season. She wanted to remember this moment as the beginning of another phase in her career, a step she'd been waiting for since she'd decided on a future in sports broadcasting.

❖

Tiernan separated a ball from the pile in front of her with the head of her eight iron and pushed it through the grass. She took a half swing and sent it sailing toward the waving flag a hundred yards away. She would spend an hour here on the range, then head over to the practice green to put in another hour.

"That was a lazy swing," Brit said from her post in the folding lawn chair to Tiernan's right. "What's on your mind?"

"I've been thinking about some of those opportunities you were talking about," Tiernan said cautiously.

"Yeah." Brit sat up straighter.

"Don't get too excited. I'm just saying I'd like to talk about them."

"What changed your mind?"

Tiernan shrugged. She pulled another ball over and hit it, but she continued to speak through her entire swing. "This revelation was so out of my control. But I have to let go of that and look forward." She paused for a moment to watch the ball's flight. She often conversed during practice as a drill in concentration and dealing with distraction. "As frustrated as I am with the way this happened, it really doesn't have to ruin my life." Tiernan thought about Elena's obvious apprehension about her brother discovering her sexuality. "I don't have family that I'm really close to who might disown me. I don't have to worry about discrimination in my workplace, because if I don't like the way I'm treated there, I can afford to leave. But some people aren't that lucky. Maybe I have a chance to make a difference for some of them."

Brit nodded. "That's a good way to look at your situation. You're not the first 'out' female athlete. But you're definitely in the minority among women golfers. You could blaze a trail for young women coming up behind you."

Tiernan shook her head. "I don't want to be set up like some type of role model. I haven't been brave. I won't pretend it was my choice to come out. But I do want to discuss what I can do to make life better for others. I've always considered that goal when

I decide where to expend my charitable energy, so it stands to reason that I should do the same in my life choices."

"Good. Personally, I think a good place to start is the ERI. They do a lot of work in support of gay marriage, anti-discrimination laws, and civil rights in general."

"How did you get to be such an authority on gay rights?"

"I've had a half dozen calls from organizations wanting your help. I did some research so I could weed out the ones that weren't legit."

"Why are they calling you and not Wally?"

"I'm more visible, I guess. Maybe I appear to be close to you and they want me to sway you. I would bet Wally's had some calls too."

"Okay. Get me the info on a couple that you think are worthwhile and I'll look them over."

"All right. Now, on to more important things. We've got a major tournament starting in three days. How do you feel about extending your winning streak?"

Tiernan laughed. "I hardly think one charity tournament is a streak."

"If they can call three losses a losing streak, I can do the same for one win."

"Are we all set to go to Maryland tomorrow? I want to get a practice round in on Wednesday." Tiernan switched to her seven iron and aimed at a different flag.

"Yeah, we're good. Our flight leaves at four p.m. You know, you could get a Palm, or a BlackBerry, or something. Then you could keep your own schedule."

"Why, when I have you?" Tiernan had a calendar at home where she kept track of her days. She checked it every morning and had a good idea of what she had going on for the next few weeks, but she often relied on Brit for the finer details of each day.

"It just wouldn't hurt you to be more organized. If something happened to me, you'd be lost."

"Don't even talk like that. It's morbid."

"I didn't necessarily mean something bad. What if I meet someone and I'm no longer able to be with you every day?" Brit stood, pulled Tiernan's six iron from her bag, and handed it to her, taking back the seven she'd been using.

"Then I guess I'll have to get a personal assistant, a trainer, and a life coach. Gee, you sure will be tough to replace."

"And expensive, too. Coaches this good won't come cheap."

"Hmm, you're probably right. It's a good thing I'll have all of the prize money from my upcoming win streak."

Brit laughed. "Okay. Don't let it go to your head. You took one charity tournament. And I think Elena did most of the work."

"She definitely had an impact." Tiernan was only half joking.

Playing with Elena had been fun—something golf hadn't been for Tiernan in longer than she realized. Sure, a best-ball tournament took some of the pressure off because they got two chances at every shot, but it was more than that. They had talked as they walked down the fairway, and not about golf. But, Tiernan now realized, they had focused mostly on her life. She still knew next to nothing about Elena's. The casual conversation had eased the pressure she'd been feeling lately during tournaments. And playing golf with Elena virtually made their competitors disappear. Tiernan hadn't been obsessed about where she and Elena were in the standings or how many birdies they needed. Instead, she had simply enjoyed challenging herself and Elena to make good shots.

CHAPTER THIRTEEN

Thursday morning, dark clouds hung heavily over Bulle Rock Golf Course as Tiernan stood on the tee box looking down the fifth hole. A difficult par four, it doglegged to the left. Tiernan had to try to place the ball in the left side of the fairway if she wanted a good look at the green for her second shot, but that meant avoiding a sand trap inside the curve.

A raindrop hit her arm as she set up for her drive, and by the time her ball landed and rolled to a stop in the fairway seconds later, it had started to sprinkle. Then the rain began in earnest. Brit opened an umbrella over them as they walked down to Tiernan's ball. Tiernan looked back over her right shoulder and found the other two players in her threesome standing near their own balls. Since she was closest to the green, she would wait for both of them to hit before she took her next shot. In the meantime, she studied her approach. She still had a hundred and eighty yards left, and since the green was uphill from where she stood, it would play more like two hundred.

Minutes later, after one of her competitors had landed on the green and the other in a trap on the right, Brit handed her a three iron.

"On the green," Tiernan said quietly to herself. She'd had a good start today, getting birdies on three of the first four holes. Water already collected on the ground so she wouldn't get as much roll after her ball landed. She swung hard. The ball landed just short of the green and bounced up. Tiernan was too far away to see exactly how close to the hole she got, but she was happy to be putting.

"The rain is really coming down. I bet they call it," Brit said as they walked up to the green.

"Damn, I hoped it would hold off so we could finish." Though weather was always a factor, Tiernan hated the interruption to her round. If a delay was called, she probably would have to sit around at least a couple of hours waiting until she could resume play.

A flash of lightning shot from the heavy clouds overhead and a crash of thunder followed only a second later. Before Tiernan could draw a breath, the horn sounded the alert that play had been suspended. A trail of people headed across the fairway in the direction of the clubhouse like a rows of ants.

"It's going to be a long day," Tiernan muttered as she walked up to her ball.

She and the other players waited for the rules officials to come over, then they marked their balls so they would know where to resume play when they returned after the delay.

By the time Tiernan left the green, Brit had loaded her clubs onto one of several golf carts that course employees were bringing out for them to ride back in. Tiernan jumped in the passenger seat and Brit took off.

"Have you heard how long it's supposed to last?" Tiernan asked.

"They say the storm is moving quickly. But I imagine they'll need at least an hour to get the course back in shape after the rain stops."

As they rounded a bend in the path between the eighth and ninth holes, Tiernan caught sight of a familiar figure.

"Pull over," she said.

"What?"

"Stop up here."

Brit slowed as they drew alongside Elena Pilar. She walked

quickly, the sweeping strides of her long legs not quite able to outrun the downpour. Wet strands of her hair stuck to her forehead and across her cheek.

"Headed in?" Tiernan realized it was a stupid question the moment she asked. Where else would Elena be going in the middle of a thunderstorm? But Tiernan used all of her concentration to keep her eyes from straying to Elena's soaked white blouse, which was almost transparent and plastered to her breasts. In the end she lost the fight and her gaze flickered lower before she jerked it up again.

Elena looked down, then crossed her arms over her chest.

"Hop on."

"No, thank you."

"Come on. Don't be silly. We're going to the same place." Tiernan scooted closer to Brit, making a small sliver of room on the seat next to her. When Elena made no move to get in, Tiernan said, "Fine. I'll walk with you. Brit, where's my umbrella?"

"Oh, all right." Elena got in, but wound up practically sitting on Tiernan's lap.

When Brit accelerated around the next bend, they were jolted toward the right side of the cart. Afraid Elena might fall out, Tiernan wrapped her arm around Elena's waist.

"Sorry," she said, even as she enjoyed the feel of Elena's body tucked against hers.

Elena didn't respond, but sat silently staring ahead as if she couldn't wait until they reached the clubhouse.

"The storm came in quickly." *God, Tiernan, you idiot, you make such stimulating conversation. It's no wonder she doesn't want to talk to you.*

Brit drove fast, alternately slamming the accelerator all the way to the floor, then the brake as she negotiated curves in the cart path. They pulled up to the back of the clubhouse and stopped behind a row of other carts.

"You guys go in and get dry. I'll get your clubs," Brit said as she leaped out and hurried around to the back of the cart.

Elena sat at an awkward angle and had to put her hand on Tiernan's thigh to leverage herself out. But as soon as she was free enough, she jerked her hand away.

"Thanks for the ride," she said politely, though she really wanted to get as far away from Tiernan as possible. Pressed against her in the cart, Elena had been able to feel the heat of Tiernan's body through their clothing. She'd barely kept herself from jumping out of the moving vehicle when Tiernan's arm came around her and her hand squeezed her side firmly. She told herself to relax. After all, she was only getting a ride in from the rain, and she had Brit as a chaperone. Surely no one would see the three of them in the cart and think anything inappropriate.

"No problem." Tiernan followed Elena into the clubhouse.

"I should go check in with my producer. They probably need some coverage during the delay."

"Of what? Golfers sitting around waiting for the storm to pass?"

"No. Of the course conditions and what's being done to get things ready to go back out after the rain."

"The rain hasn't stopped yet." Tiernan took Elena's elbow and steered her toward the locker room. "You probably have time to put some dry clothes on first."

"I didn't bring any other clothes." As usual, she had checked the forecast several times that morning before she left her hotel room. But since the Weather Channel hadn't called for anything other than partly cloudy skies, Elena hadn't packed any provisions.

"I have some you can borrow."

Elena allowed Tiernan to lead her through the door, but her stomach knotted nervously as she thought about being naked and alone with Tiernan. Of course, if she'd been thinking clearly, she would have realized that an entire field of golfers had just come in from the rain. And when they entered the locker room, it seemed as if every one of them was in there at the same time trying to change clothes. She needn't have worried about being alone with Tiernan.

Tiernan threaded her way through the crowd of women, all of whom seemed to be offering their opinion on the rain delay. She opened a locker and immediately began to pull clothes out of a duffle bag. She handed Elena a pair of navy blue nylon warm-up pants and a jacket.

"They may be a little big, but they're dry and will keep the rain off you if you have to go back out there."

As Elena unfolded the jacket, she discovered the Spin Golf Apparel logo on the front. Tiernan glanced up and smiled.

"Well, they wanted you to wear their stuff, right?"

Elena had been thinking that anyone who saw her would have little doubt where she'd gotten her clothes. God, when did she become so paranoid? Spin was a popular company and she wouldn't be the only one wearing their clothes. Besides, just because Tiernan was a lesbian didn't mean anyone who associated with her was. Elena had always hated that type of blanket assumption and now she was making one herself.

Elena undressed, then quickly put on the clothes Tiernan had given her. She avoided looking at Tiernan, because even though she didn't want anyone to assume she was a lesbian, the fact remained that she was. And, she *was* attracted to Tiernan. So even in a room full of people, she didn't trust herself to catch even a glimpse of Tiernan as she too changed into dry clothes. But she was still extremely aware of her. Tiernan stood close enough in the crowded space that Elena could smell the floral scent of her damp hair.

"Thanks again for the clothes. I'll get them back to you tomorrow. I really do need to check in with my producer." Elena hurried from the room before Tiernan could reply. She would need to be careful around Tiernan. A crush on a very publicly out golfer was the last thing Elena needed right now.

❖

"David, it looks like the rain has stopped, at least for now. The grounds crew has dispersed with the squeegees trying to get the water out of these greens so they can resume play. But the latest from league officials indicates they won't start until after lunch." Elena waited until the cameraman signaled that they had cut back to the booth announcers before she relaxed her smile.

"Thank you, Elena," David said in her earpiece. "The good news is, the forecast for tomorrow is sunny skies."

"Okay, guys." This time the voice belonged to Cindy. "Take a break. The network has arranged to rerun some old footage. Keep your cell on, and I'll call you if we need you to do an update."

Elena checked to make sure her phone was on, then pulled the earpiece out and tucked it inside the collar of her shirt. The cameraman was halfway across the grass before Cindy finished speaking. Elena walked back to the clubhouse more slowly. Now that the rain had stopped she didn't need to hurry. The clubhouse was packed with people, no doubt waiting impatiently to get back out there, whereas Elena had the course pretty much to herself right now.

She had chosen to do her report in front of the ninth green so the grounds keepers could be seen working in the background. She strolled over to the tree-lined drive that led from the main road to the clubhouse. As she walked on the edge of it, under a canopy of trees, water dripped in fat drops from the tips of leaves heavy with rain. The sun was trying to break through the clouds, but for the meantime, the saturated flora around her seemed even more vividly colored beneath the overcast sky.

"Are you done working?"

Elena had been so intent on her surroundings that she was startled to see Tiernan step out from behind a tree about five yards ahead of her.

"For now. When they get closer to a start time, I'll be busy again."

"So until then you're just enjoying this beautiful weather?"

"Now that the rain has stopped it's kind of nice out here."

"Do you mind if I join you, then?" Tiernan fell into step beside Elena without waiting for a response.

When they reached an intersection between the main road and a cart path, Elena turned right and headed toward the eighteenth hole.

"So, is it just you and Vincent, or do you have any other siblings?"

The question, blurted into the silence, startled Elena. "Just us."

"I know he mentioned children. Do you have any?"

"No. What is this?"

"What?"

"This—" she waved her hand between them—"all of the questions."

Tiernan shrugged. "I realized I talked a lot about myself last week, but you didn't talk about you. Or I didn't ask, I guess."

"There's not much interesting to tell, really."

"Well, for starters, I heard you and Vincent speaking Spanish. Where are you from?"

"Orlando."

"No. I mean, originally."

"Orlando."

"Oh."

Elena smiled. "My parents are from Puerto Rico, and my brother was born there, but I was born in Orlando. We're both fluent in Spanish because our parents made sure we spoke both languages. It's a habit sometimes when we're together."

"Were they proud of your performance in the tournament last week?"

Elena shrugged. Though her family had taken her to dinner and acted excited, she suspected it was mostly because they knew the opportunity had mattered to her. "I guess. I don't think they really understood why I was so excited about—"

"About what?"

"Nothing."

"Come on." Tiernan touched the inside of Elena's elbow, then lightly pinched her side. Elena yelped and jerked away. Tiernan grinned. "Tell me. What were you excited about?"

"You."

"Me?" Tiernan stopped in the middle of the cart path. Her expression changed, her eyes darkened to a deep cobalt, and her lids grew heavy with desire. Elena shivered under the intensity of her gaze.

"Yes. I mean, I looked forward to playing with you. I thought I might learn something."

"You should have told me that." Tiernan hadn't taken her eyes off Elena. "I definitely could have taught you a thing or two, if I'd known that's what you wanted."

The innuendo in her words was unmistakable, but Elena chose to ignore it. "Actually, I did learn a lot from you."

"Well, it certainly wasn't how to lose graciously."

"I almost learned how to read a putt," Elena deadpanned.

Tiernan laughed. "Well, while playing with you, *I* was reminded of something I'd forgotten."

"Yeah? What's that?" Elena resumed walking, leading them around the bleachers at the eighteenth green.

"That golf can be fun."

"You'd forgotten that?"

"You sound surprised."

"If I played golf for a living, I would thank my lucky stars every day to have such a great job. You do what most people wish they could do while they're sitting in a cubicle somewhere for eight hours a day."

"Well, I'm not going to say I wish I was in their cubicle. But there's a lot they probably don't think about. Interviews, endorsements, pressure…and, you still think I have a dream job and I'm just a whiner." Tiernan gave a self-effacing smile. "That's probably true. I know I've got it good. Really, I do. But it's easy to forget how much fun it can be to just *play* the game—when there's nothing else riding on it, nothing at stake but an afternoon's pleasure."

"Then I'm glad I reminded you of that."

"And you reminded me that I can enjoy spending time with a woman, getting to know someone new." Tiernan brushed her hand against the back of Elena's.

"Tiernan, I don't think it's a good idea for us to get involved." Elena wanted to take Tiernan's hand, but was afraid of the mixed message she would be sending. A part of her wanted to draw closer to Tiernan while another part said to push her away. "I can't."

"Why? I'm only talking about dinner."

Elena sighed. "Because you are very out and extremely public. And I'm not ready to make that kind of statement."

Tiernan smiled to herself. What was it about Elena that made her keep setting herself up for rejection? Elena had made it clear she wasn't interested, and instead of letting it go and moving on, Tiernan needed to understand her reasons. "So I wasn't totally off base. I mean, there's something here, right? At least tell me you're a lesbian, so I don't feel like a total idiot."

"It's complicated."

"What's complicated? Either you like girls or you like boys. Or you like both, and there's a word for that too."

"All right. If you want a label, I would say I am a lesbian. But I haven't dated anyone since college. I haven't let myself."

"Because of your parents?"

Elena nodded. "They have very traditional values. And it's not just them. It's my job, too. I might have missed out on a lot of opportunities as an out-and-proud lesbian. I'd probably still be covering junior golf."

"Times are changing." And this was one of the reasons that Tiernan needed to get involved in affecting her community. It was a shame for a woman like Elena to remain single and celibate simply because she was afraid of what she'd risk in her career and with her family.

"They aren't changing that fast, Tiernan. Broadcasting is still a man's world."

"There are other women sportscasters."

"In golf that usually means they used to play professionally and have the clout to get a position." Elena grimaced. "I'm not trying to whine about my job, either. All I'm saying is that I have my reasons for shying away from relationships, specifically one with a high-profile athlete."

"Point taken." Tiernan wanted to argue, but she sensed Elena's mind was made up. "Can we be friends? Or is that off-limits, too?"

"We can be friendly."

Tiernan wasn't entirely sure what the distinction was, but she suspected Elena still wanted to keep her distance. However, the door was opening, even if only a tiny bit. It might be interesting to step inside and see what happened.

CHAPTER FOURTEEN

TIERNAN O'SHEA SNAPS LOSING STREAK WITH RUNAWAY WIN AT BULLE ROCK

Tiernan read the headline one more time. Beneath it was a black-and-white photo of her kissing a large silver urn. She'd been fairly far ahead of the pack for most of the tournament and no one had really come out to challenge her, so she rode her lead all the way to Sunday afternoon.

She had just arrived home from Maryland, and after she finished her laundry she would start packing again. She needed to be in Pittsford, New York, tomorrow for the next tournament. Kim had grown to hate all the traveling, but she never agreed when Tiernan suggested she go alone and Kim stay home. For Tiernan the travel wasn't a big deal, just part of the job. But even though Kim had seen how much work and how little play those trips were for Tiernan, she still didn't trust her.

This week Tiernan was actually looking forward to the trip, because she knew she would run into Elena. Perhaps it was winning again that made her relax enough to spend time thinking about Elena. Her relationship with Kim had been convenient. They'd both understood that they needed to hide who they were. And if Tiernan were the same person she was then, perhaps she could convince Elena to carry on the same type of affair. But for Tiernan that was no longer an option. In the past, it hadn't been a big deal for her assistant to be seen everywhere with her. But now, the press would speculate about any woman with whom Tiernan spent time regularly. She could not offer Elena the anonymity she thought she needed.

Instead, Tiernan probably should steer clear of Elena Pilar. But remembering her silky hair and dark, mysterious eyes, her sensuous curves and the way her smile spread warmth through Tiernan's body, she knew staying away wouldn't be easy.

The ringing phone interrupted her thoughts before she could venture too far into a fantasy about Elena. She glanced at the caller I.D., then pressed the button to answer.

"Hey, Wally."

"Hey, kid. Good show this weekend."

"Thanks."

"I got a call from the folks at Spin and they said to pass along their congratulations as well."

"Yeah? Are they satisfied?" Tiernan picked up the paper and read the headline again.

"For now."

Tiernan laughed. "Of course. Unless I lose this weekend, right?"

"But you're not going to lose, are you?"

"No, sir. The plan is for a win again this week."

"They might be happy with top five."

"Well, I do play to please them," Tiernan said sarcastically. "On another note, Brit had some ideas I want to discuss with you. She's been contacted by some organizations that want me to do some promotion with them."

"Some more exposure couldn't hurt you right now."

"Well, the catch is, these are gay and lesbian organizations."

"I think it's a good idea."

"You do?" She hadn't expected his response. She had assumed his feelings on homosexuality were negative.

"Sure. Your orientation is already out there. In fact, it's

almost old news. And since you don't plan to deny it or try to hide it, why not take control of it? Why should the tabloids be the only ones to benefit?"

Tiernan finally understood his motivation. In his business, dollar signs trumped personal values every time. "Okay. I'll go over the information Brit gave me and pick out the ones I like. I'll fax you the details on those and you can set something up."

"Sounds good. And you know, like everything else, once the media puts your new activities out there, some other opportunities will come along."

"I know." Tiernan understood the power of the press all too well. "I'm making a choice here, Wally. I can either act like nothing has changed and attempt to keep everything private, or I can use my celebrity to try to positively affect the world and others like me. When I think about it that way, it seems kind of selfish not to."

❖

Elena stood at the window of her second-floor hotel room. The pool below was empty. In fact, except for one occupant the entire patio area was vacant. The lone sunbather was stretched out on a lounge. Her sunglasses, a poor disguise, covered her eyes, but there was no mistaking that cap of blond hair, the long torso left bare by her light blue two-piece swimsuit, or those firm, muscled thighs. Judging by the sheen of sweat Elena thought she could make out on Tiernan's stomach, it must be pretty hot outside. Now that she thought about it, a dip in the pool did sound nice.

She just wanted a refreshing swim, at least that's what she told herself as she slipped into a swimsuit, grabbed a towel, and rode the elevator to the ground floor. Once there, she hesitated for a moment, wondering if she should go back upstairs. A swim, an innocent swim. She forged ahead, intent that her motives were pure.

When she stepped onto the patio, she knew purity was not foremost in her mind. Up close, Tiernan was even more tempting. She looked so relaxed, stretched out on the chaise, that Elena wondered if she was asleep. Her skin glistened as if from the effort of drawing energy from the sun overhead.

"Place is kind of deserted for such a nice day, isn't it?" Elena said to announce herself as she ventured closer.

Tiernan lifted her head and looked at Elena. "Were you hoping for better company?"

"Not at all."

Tiernan shifted in her chaise, sitting up straighter. "The hotel is full of golfers. I suspect they're all at the course practicing for tomorrow's round."

"Why aren't you?" Elena pulled her T-shirt over her head and draped it on the back of the chair next to Tiernan's.

"I've practiced enough. If I don't know how to do it now, I never will." Tiernan's eyes dipped to Elena's chest, and Elena fought the urge to cover her brief bikini top.

"That's a new attitude for you, isn't it?"

"I'm trying it out. We'll see tomorrow how it works."

"Keep me posted." Elena pushed her shorts over her hips and stepped out of them. She moved quickly to the pool because Tiernan's gaze made her nervous.

She dove in and when she resurfaced, Tiernan still watched her. Needing to put some distance between them, she turned onto her stomach and swam the length of the pool.

Tiernan walked around the pool's edge and Elena slowed her pace and rolled to her back. Tiernan smiled and met her eyes as she stepped onto the diving board. She turned around and stood on the end of the board, her heels even with the edge. She raised her arms and in one smooth motion launched herself backward and flipped into the pool. Elena held her breath until Tiernan surfaced. She swam to the ladder, climbed out, and returned to the diving board. This time she stood at the back of the board and took two quick steps before planting her hands on the surface and pushing off, dropping into the water feet first. She came up only a foot away from where Elena was treading water.

"Impressive."

"It suddenly got hot out here, and I needed to cool off."

"Did it work?"

"It was refreshing." Tiernan's gaze fell to Elena's breasts, just beneath the surface of the water. "But I'm still pretty hot."

"You know, I would slap a man for leering at me like that."

Tiernan grinned, and when she pulled her eyes back to Elena's face, she didn't see any apology in them. "Are you going to slap me?"

"I should."

Tiernan swam back a couple feet, out of reach. "Come and get me."

"I thought we agreed we were going to be friendly." Elena couldn't help smiling. She enjoyed the teasing banter.

"Oh, I want to be very friendly."

Heat swirled low in Elena's stomach and between her thighs at the desire in Tiernan's voice and on her face. Tiernan wanted her, and she wasn't trying to hide it. Reciprocal lust surged up in Elena, and though she knew she should, suppressing it was a struggle for her. When Tiernan swam toward her, with that same hunger in her eyes, Elena retreated. But Ticrnan didn't stop advancing until Elena felt the smooth tile of the pool's side against her back.

"We can't," she said weakly when a slow smile slid across Tiernan's lips.

Tiernan closed the distance, bracing her arms on either side of Elena. However, somehow Elena knew that they weren't holding her captive, that if she tried she could move Tiernan's arm and escape. She could escape this moment, but not the fire building inside.

When Tiernan moved closer and pressed her body against her, Elena valiantly fought the urge to wrap her arms around Tiernan's back. But she lost the battle as Tiernan's lips descended on hers and caressed them softly at first, then more urgently. She clutched Tiernan's shoulders, her fingers slipping against Tiernan's wet skin. When Tiernan's teeth scraped against her lips, Elena moaned.

A distant voice pulled Elena from her fog of desire and she shoved against Tiernan's shoulders, pushing her back enough to separate their lips.

"Someone could come out here any time," Elena said between panting breaths. She needed the reminder as much as Tiernan did.

"I don't care."

"I'm sorry. I do." Elena pushed Tiernan's arm out of the way and swam toward the ladder.

Her body hummed with the desire to stay in the pool, but she forced herself to climb out. On shaky legs she strode to the chaise and picked up her towel and discarded clothes. She didn't dare glance at Tiernan, but she thought she could feel her eyes on her. She waited until she got in the hallway to quickly step into her shorts and tug on her T-shirt.

You got what you deserve. The voice in her head offered no forgiveness. She'd gone down to the pool knowing she was tempting herself, and she'd failed to deny herself the pleasure of a kiss. Even if only momentary, it was a lapse, nonetheless.

Elena was still thinking about that kiss the next morning, as she walked along the cart path to the eighteenth green. Her cameraman had gotten a ride with his equipment a few minutes earlier, but Elena preferred to walk. She'd awakened that morning amid a strange dream in which she was the one pursuing Tiernan. As her alarm pealed, she clung to the memory of Tiernan's kiss, and she wished she could say she felt more regret. Instead of being sorry she'd allowed things to go that far, she actually wondered how it would have felt to keep kissing Tiernan, to let

Tiernan press her against the edge of the pool and slip her hand between them.

No. She banished the wet, steamy image. She'd pushed Tiernan away and she would *not* use her as fodder for her fantasies. Her focus today should be on her job, not on Tiernan O'Shea. In fact, she vowed, the only time she would think about Tiernan today was when her pairing came up to the green, and then only so long as to read her putt.

She didn't even come close to keeping that promise. Every time they had to wait a few minutes for another twosome to approach, she caught herself thinking about playing golf with Tiernan, or the sexy way she smiled, or the surprisingly elegant movements of her hands when she gestured while she talked. Or worse yet, one time she relived that kiss and the moments leading up to it, and she had to cross her arms over her chest as she felt her nipples pucker beneath her thin polo. Each time she chastised herself and forced her mind back to the play of golfers who were not Tiernan.

Tiernan's group was one of the last to come up the fairway, and in spite of her attempt at resolve, Elena's heartbeat accelerated when she caught sight of her a hundred yards away. Tiernan was setting up for her approach shot, and Elena was so intent on watching her that she nearly missed a question from the booth.

"It should be an easy pitch for her from there, David." Elena hoped David hadn't been aware of her distraction a moment ago. "Today's hole position is up on that shelf at the back of this green. She wants to land it up there or she'll be left with a difficult putt."

Elena was certain Tiernan could make this shot from a hundred feet directly in front of the green with her eyes closed. Only two weeks ago, she'd seen her drop a similar one onto the green twenty feet closer than the shot Elena had attempted.

With a three-quarter swing of what Elena guessed was a pitching wedge, Tiernan struck the ball cleanly. It landed on top of the ridge that ran across the center of the green.

"That was well done. What does she have left, Elena?" David asked.

"That's right where she wanted to put this ball. She'll have a nice birdie attempt."

Elena watched Tiernan hand her wedge back to Brit and take her putter. They walked up the fairway together, no doubt discussing this final putt. Tiernan lifted her head and Elena felt like she was looking right at her. But she was still too far away to pick Elena out in the crowd of media around her. More likely she was checking her standing on the huge leaderboard behind them. Elena didn't need to look to know that Tiernan was one point off the lead. If she sank this putt she would go into tomorrow's round tied for first.

As Tiernan stepped onto the green, she scanned the gallery crowding behind the roped-off area nearby. When her gaze passed over the media section, then stopped and returned, there was no mistaking this time; she was looking at Elena. Elena felt her face flush and hoped no one around her noticed. Tiernan smiled and lifted her chin slightly, and Elena couldn't help smiling back, though she quickly bent her head to hide the expression.

Tiernan appeared to shift focus quickly as she crouched near her ball. Eyes that a moment ago seemed to be flirting with Elena were now intensely concentrated on the path of her next shot.

"This is a straight putt, David. It won't do much of anything." Elena's attempt to force herself back to business wasn't as successful as she predicted Tiernan's shot would be, and she hoped the breathlessness she felt wasn't evident in her voice.

With a confident stroke, Tiernan rolled the ball in. She bent to retrieve it and handed it and her putter to Brit. Without waiting for Brit, Tiernan strode across the green, headed for the opening in the crowd between the media section and other spectators. Beyond them, she would find the scorekeepers' tent. While the others around Elena shouted questions, she stood silently as Tiernan's eyes locked on her.

Too late, she realized that Tiernan intended to stop for

an interview. She ignored Elena's peers and looked at Elena expectantly. Searching her suddenly befuddled mind for a question, Elena drew on an old standby.

"You shot a sixty-seven today, ending the round at five under par and tied for the lead. What do you need to do for the rest of the weekend to pull out a win?"

Tiernan rubbed a hand over the bill of her hat and Elena tracked the motion of her strong, slender fingers as if she were the one sighting a ball. Tiernan smiled as if she knew exactly the effect she had on Elena.

"I just need to play solid golf. I definitely could have had a few more scoring opportunities—could have made a few more putts. We played short of the creek on thirteen, which I think was a safe bet, but tomorrow I'd like to go for it there."

Another reporter jumped in with her own question. "You're tied with tour rookie Regina Paine, who has been a surprisingly strong force early this year. How would you size up her game in comparison to your own?"

"Regina is a strong player. I've been paired with her a couple of times already this year. But I intend to go out and play my own round and not worry about what anyone else is doing." Tiernan didn't look at the other reporter when she answered the question. Her eyes never left Elena.

"She beat you at Kingsmill. That defeat won't be in the back of your mind this weekend?"

"It might now," Tiernan joked. "No, seriously, I'm only worried about my performance. If I play the way I know I can and she still ends up scoring better, then I guess she deserves the win." Tiernan ignored several more questions. "Thanks, guys. I'll see you all tomorrow."

Tiernan smiled and walked away.

"O'Shea seems in unusually good spirits today, Elena," David said in her ear.

"Yes, she seems to be pleased with her round and looking forward to the rest of the weekend." Elena didn't know what else to say. Tiernan did seem to have changed, but Elena wasn't about to speculate with David about why.

"It's more than that. She's relaxed and approaching her game differently somehow. It's like she's…well, I don't know how else to say it except she seems like she's having fun."

"Ah, well, of course, she is. She's winning."

Elena was glad when he accepted the joke as a response and moved on to his postgame wrap-up and predictions for the remainder of the tournament. Since Elena wasn't expected to offer her opinion during this segment of the show, she helped her cameraman pack up his gear, then headed toward the clubhouse.

CHAPTER FIFTEEN

Tiernan rolled over Sunday morning and slammed her hand against the top of the alarm clock on the nightstand. She lay amid the stiff white hotel sheets and smiled at the ceiling. She was having a very good weekend and today, the final round of the tournament, would cap it off. She pushed back the covers and padded naked to the adjoining bathroom to turn on the shower.

Once inside, she let the hot water cascade over her while her mind wandered back over the past two days. She'd gone into Friday's round tied with Regina and finished that day two shots ahead. Saturday, she extended her lead and would begin today's round five strokes up. She needed to play clean though, because that was not an insurmountable lead. If Tiernan made a few mistakes, Regina could capitalize and come back. Before she went to sleep last night, Tiernan had played the round in her head, imagining places where she could take some chances while still protecting her lead. But in the end, it would come down to feel and instinct.

After she finished dressing, Tiernan headed for the elevator. No matter what city she was in, she liked to eat breakfast downstairs instead of in her room. She would choose a seat in the corner of the café or restaurant and spend a half hour people watching while she ate.

Today she found her corner seat already occupied, but she

only became more determined to sit there. Across the dining room, Elena was intent on the newspaper in front of her and didn't notice Tiernan as she wove between the tables.

"Mind if I join you?" Tiernan sat without waiting for an answer. She didn't want to give Elena a chance to say no.

"Actually, I was just leaving."

Elena closed and folded her newspaper, but before Elena could make a move to stand up, a waitress placed a full plate of food in front of her.

"Can I get you anything?" she asked Tiernan.

Tiernan looked at Elena's plate then back at the waitress. "I'll have what she's having, but orange juice instead of coffee."

"So, you were leaving before you got your food?" Tiernan asked after the waitress had left.

"I guess not." Elena folded her hands in her lap.

"Please, go ahead and eat while it's hot." Tiernan reached across the table and slid the newspaper out from under the edge of Elena's plate. She unfolded it and scanned the front page.

Elena picked up her fork and Tiernan continued to act as if engrossed in the paper, but she was covertly studying Elena.

The waitress brought Tiernan's juice, and as she sipped it, she wondered what someone observing them might think. Elena was intent on her breakfast and Tiernan on the paper and neither spoke. Did they look like a couple used to spending the morning hour together? Did Tiernan want to become used to spending her mornings with Elena?

"Are you on eighteen again?" Tiernan asked.

"Yes."

"I'll be sure to stop by and talk to you after I finish." Tiernan had sought Elena out at the end of her round for each of the past three days. But for some reason, Elena hadn't capitalized on the attention and offered only a few common questions before allowing someone else to jump in.

"Why?"

"Because I enjoy seeing you."

"That's not a good enough reason."

"No? Well, I don't know what else to tell you." How would Elena react to the complete truth? Tiernan liked coming off the green and seeing Elena's face. She wanted to pretend that Elena was there to watch her play, not that she was simply doing her job. "If I'm going to give an interview to someone, why shouldn't it be you?"

"It'll become obvious that you're singling me out, if it's not already."

"And what will people think," Tiernan finished for her. "God forbid they think you're a lesbian." Tiernan leaned forward, bracing her biceps against the edge of the table, and lowered her voice. "What would they think if they knew how much I really want to kiss you again?"

Elena paused with her fork halfway to her mouth, clearly remembering their kiss. It had obviously rattled Elena as much as it had her.

"So, that whole lounging-by-the-pool-instead-of-practicing thing worked out for you, huh?" Elena ignored Tiernan's comment and changed the subject.

"It appears so." Tiernan straightened in her chair as the waitress brought her food. "And I have you to thank."

"Me? Why?"

Tiernan laid her napkin across her lap. "Playing in that tournament with you turned my luck around."

"How much luck do you really think is involved?"

"A little." Tiernan shrugged. "Mostly, you reminded me why I kept playing in the first place. For as long as I can remember, my dad wanted me to be a golfer. He put a club in my hand before I even knew what it was, so of course it was never my decision to start playing. He had me practicing for hours a day. After school, while my friends were playing team sports, I was on the range by myself hitting bucket after bucket.

"Don't get me wrong, I love the game. It was all worth it and I wouldn't trade where I am now for anything. My point is, he always tried to make practice fun. He made up little games and challenges for me. Being on the range or out on the course with my dad was a blast. I lost some of that when he died. On my own, I forgot that I needed to enjoy what I was doing. And the other day, being out there with you, I felt like I used to in some ways. I was able to forget about the competition and enjoy the game again. It's been a long time…so I need to thank you for that." Talking about her father always made her emotional, and Tiernan swallowed to get rid of the thickness in her throat.

"Wow. I don't know what to say, Tiernan."

"You don't need to say anything." Tiernan cleared her throat. "I didn't mean to get into all that."

"No. I'm glad you did. And I'm so glad you were able to recapture that feeling. Hold on to it."

"Yeah, well." The conversation had become more personal than Tiernan wanted. She threw enough bills to cover both of their meals on the table and stood. "I'll see you out there in a few hours."

"Yes. Good luck. And, Tiernan—" Elena stood as well— "please, don't single me out for any more interviews."

"Come on, don't you want to interview the tournament winner this afternoon?" Tiernan grinned and strode away without waiting for a reply. The question was a bit cockier than she would normally have been going into the fourth round, but Elena's request had irritated her and she'd reacted with hurt feelings.

Six hours later, through her earpiece, Elena heard David and Bobby commenting on Tiernan's drive on eighteen.

"She's smoked it down the middle of this narrow fairway."

Tiernan's ball rolled to a stop in the fairway a hundred yards from the green in about the same place as she'd been in each of the previous rounds. Then, minutes later, Regina's ball bounced on the left edge of the fairway, into the rough and under a tree. She would have a tough time getting on in two from there. But at this point it didn't matter. Mathematically, Regina couldn't catch Tiernan, and the third-place player was so far behind her that, barring a disaster, she would hold onto second.

Tiernan pitched her ball onto the green knowing she'd sewn up the tournament. Regina left her second shot short, then chipped close to the flag and putted in to save her par. Tiernan sank a long putt to end with a birdie.

As the players and their caddies came off the green, Elena saw Tiernan heading in her direction again.

"Get the interview with O'Shea," Cindy said in Elena's ear.

But when Tiernan was within a few feet of her, Elena took a step to the right, putting another reporter between them, then another step brought her out on the other side and directly in front of Regina Paine.

"Regina, can I have a word?" she asked quickly.

"Sure."

"I've got Regina," Elena said into her mic to clue David and Bobby in on her intro. She waited only a minute until she heard them go to her, then her cameramen signaled that they were on.

"I'm here with Regina Paine, who has just turned in a four-under-par round for the day, leaving her three under to take second in the tournament. You had a great round today, Regina, and really executed well all week. You've been top five in the last six tournaments. As a rookie on the tour, you've got to be ecstatic with the way you've been performing these last several weeks."

"Yes, absolutely. There's a lot of good competition out here. Playing with golfers of this caliber tests the nerves, for sure. I had some pretty good shots this week, but Tiernan just finished better. She's pretty amazing."

Elena wanted to agree, but instead stayed centered on

Regina. "Well, you handle the pressure well. You're unflappable out there. How do you stay so focused?"

"I just try to play my game and not worry what anyone else is doing." Regina smiled, a brilliant flash of white, full of enthusiasm.

"It's working for you. Good luck next week." Elena smiled back. "Bobby, I'll send it back to you for the postgame." After her cameraman lowered his camera and turned away, Elena turned to Regina and put out her hand. "Thanks for the interview."

"My pleasure." Regina grasped Elena's hand firmly and held it for a moment. She looked as if she wanted to say something else, but someone over Elena's shoulder caught her attention. "I've got to go." She released Elena's hand. "I'll see you around."

"What the hell was that? I told you to get O'Shea." Elena cringed at the disappointment in Cindy's voice.

"I missed her. So I grabbed Paine." Elena knew the excuse would work only if her cameraman kept his mouth shut. He couldn't have missed seeing her sidestep Tiernan.

Still several feet away, Tiernan had finished her interview with a rival network and waved off several more reporters. As Elena and her cameraman headed for the clubhouse, Tiernan intercepted her.

"Hey, how about that interview now?"

The cameraman heard her and started to swing his camera onto his shoulder.

"I don't think so."

He cast Elena a disbelieving look.

"We've already gone into our postgame show."

He shook his head and walked away.

Watching him go, Elena said, "That probably blows any chance of him not telling Cindy." She resumed walking toward the clubhouse.

"Telling her what?" Tiernan fell into step beside her.

"Nothing. Don't you have a trophy to accept?"

"I need to turn in my scorecard first. And I can't go too far from the tent, so please hold up for a second." Tiernan grabbed Elena's elbow to stop her.

"I told you I'm not going to interview you."

"Still worried someone will see us on television and guess that you're a lesbian?"

The entire time Tiernan had been talking to the other reporter, she'd kept her head turned so that she could watch the exchange between Elena and Regina. An odd curl of jealousy within her had thrown her. She didn't get jealous—ever. Her reaction was irrational, because neither Elena nor Regina acted inappropriately. But for some reason, seeing Elena smiling at Regina inspired envy in Tiernan. The people Elena talked with probably considered her warmth an asset, but it only made Tiernan wish Elena would focus her attention on her.

"Keep your voice down, please," Elena snapped.

"Have dinner with me tonight."

"No."

"You managed to avoid me this afternoon, so maybe I'll take the hint and not give you any more interviews. Even when I win." It was a dirty trick, but Tiernan was desperate to spend more time with Elena. Besides, she had no intention of following through on the threat, but Elena didn't need to know that. "How many times can you talk to the second-place player before your producer gets on your case?"

"You wouldn't dare."

"Have dinner with me."

"That's blackmail."

"Elena, one dinner. If you prefer not to be seen in public with me, we can have it in my hotel room. I promise to behave. And whatever the outcome, I'll play fair for the rest of the season."

"Okay. One dinner. Tonight at seven in your room. But I can't stay late. I have an early flight."

"Good. I'll see you then. I'm in Room 231."

Tiernan walked into the tent to turn in her scorecard, suppressing the urge to whistle. She checked her scores and signed the card. In about fifteen minutes the tournament officials would be ready for the trophy presentation. And though it felt great to record another win, Tiernan was anticipating her evening with Elena even more.

CHAPTER SIXTEEN

Tiernan stepped out of the shower and wrapped a towel around herself. She squeezed a dab of gel into her hand and rubbed her fingers through her hair, checking her reflection in the steam-streaked mirror. With thirty minutes left until Elena arrived, Tiernan took her time thumbing through the hangers in the closet. Eventually, she chose khakis and a blue button-down that she'd been told matched her eyes perfectly. She slid her favorite platinum ring on her finger and fastened a Movado watch on her wrist. She sprayed on a bit of her favorite scent.

With fifteen minutes to spare, she called room service and placed an order she hoped would be perfectly timed to arrive after she and Elena had a chance to get comfortable. She'd just finished picking up some clothes, throwing them in the closet, and straightening her room when she heard a knock at the door.

She swung the door open to find Elena on the other side, looking less than happy about their evening.

"I'm here. Will you stop with the threats now?" Elena's scowl couldn't detract from her beauty. The sunny yellow of her halter-style dress contrasted nicely with her golden skin and the silky curtain of hair that fell past her bare shoulders.

"Wow. Suddenly, I feel underdressed."

Elena flushed. When she'd put the dress on she knew it might be too much for dinner in a hotel room, but in the end she decided to wear it because it was her favorite. And the expression on Tiernan's face made the decision worth it.

"Come in, please."

Elena stepped past Tiernan and was relieved to find that she had a suite and they would be dining in the outer room. She'd worried they might spend the evening adjacent to Tiernan's bed. Elena wasn't certain how long she could resist thoughts of Tiernan sprawled across that bed. She still wasn't sure why she had accepted Tiernan's invitation, but it wasn't because of Tiernan's attempt at blackmail. She might have been in hot water with Cindy, but she wouldn't compromise her job to stay out of trouble. When it came down to it, she had to admit she was here because she wanted to be.

"Please, sit." Tiernan gestured toward the loveseat and chair that formed a conversation area in front of the television.

Elena sat on one end of the loveseat and, as she expected, Tiernan settled on the other end.

"I'm sorry about the way I persuaded you to come here. That was unfair."

Elena smiled. "It's a little late to apologize now, isn't it?"

"I suppose so. Would you like to leave?" Tiernan was teasing her, and Elena liked it.

"I *am* rather hungry. Since I'm here, I may as well let you feed me."

"I'm happy to." Tiernan crossed one leg over the other.

"Congratulations on your win today. You really seem to have turned things around."

"Just in time, too. But I learned a valuable lesson in loyalty. You deserve some kudos, too, for extending your time with us on the tour."

"Thank you. I just wonder how much of that was due to my connection to you."

"What? One accident that happened weeks ago. No. They kept you on because you're good at what you do."

"Thank you. I hope it leads to more time working professional tournaments, even after this season."

"You've really never had aspirations to play?"

"None. My interest was always in broadcasting. In fact, for a time I thought I might do some work in football."

"Really? I can't picture you standing in the middle of a bunch of huge guys in pads and helmets. So you're a football fan?"

"If it weren't for having to work some tournaments on Sundays, I'd be a fanatic. Until I started covering the golf team, I didn't miss a game in college. But all of the guys on my college radio station staff fought over who got to work the football games, and no one wanted to work golf matches. So I volunteered."

"I guess I should thank all of those guys who loved watching a bunch of no-neck brutes knock each other down."

"Not a fan, huh?"

"Not really. Golf is so much more civilized."

Their dinner arrived, and after the waiter left, Tiernan lifted a bottle from an ice bucket on the cart.

"Wine? I hope red is okay."

"It's good, thank you."

Tiernan poured two glasses and began to uncover trays of food. "I didn't know what you liked so I ordered both steak and chicken and some salads."

"It all smells good. How can I help?" Elena stood and crossed the room.

"You can sit over here." Tiernan pulled out one of the chairs at the small dinette table situated along one wall. She wheeled the cart closer to the table and placed a salad in front of each of them, then sat across from Elena.

They chatted amiably as they worked their way through each course, sharing stories of their very different childhoods. Elena talked about the fusion of growing up in a traditional Puerto Rican home and attending a very American high school in Orlando.

Tiernan was fascinated by Elena's accounts of her family's

culture and how her parents strove to instill their traditional values in two impressionable young children who were often wooed by their friends' material possessions.

Her own tales mostly revolved around her father and golf. As she talked, she realized how absent from her life her mother had been and still was. Had her mother felt left out of the goals Tiernan and her father shared, or was she satisfied with the scope of their relationship? Her mother had never understood her father's drive to make Tiernan into a professional athlete any more than she now understood Tiernan's passion for the game. When Tiernan had spoken to her shortly after the media nightmare with Kim, she hadn't grasped how afraid Tiernan was of losing her career. Tiernan got angry when her mother accused her of being overly dramatic, even though she was partly right. Of course, at the time, Tiernan had been too wrapped up in her own trauma to think about the feelings that might have resurfaced for her mother. God, her mother would have a fit if she knew Tiernan was interested in a reporter.

When they finished dinner, Tiernan loaded the plates back on the cart and wheeled it into the hallway.

"That's one good thing about hotel living. I never have to do dishes."

"I solve that problem by not cooking, much to my mother's horror." Elena moved back to the loveseat.

"I love to cook. I just don't get a chance very often." Tiernan sat down next to her. "And now, when I am at home it seems a waste of time to cook for just myself. It's a lot easier to eat a bowl of cereal."

"Cereal?"

"Oh, yeah. I could live on Cinnamon Toast Crunch."

"I've never had it."

"What? You really do live a deprived life."

"Do you get more than a day or two at home often?" Elena tucked her legs underneath her.

"Not usually during the season. When I have some free

time, Wally schedules me for promotional stuff for the league and photo shoots. During the winter, I might play one tournament a month, so I get to be home more."

Elena smiled. "And you probably spend most of that time training or practicing."

"That's true." Tiernan stretched her arm along the back of the loveseat. "But it's what I love to do. Besides, it won't always be that way. There's more to life than golf."

"I can't believe you said that." Elena laughed. "Like what?"

"Like home and family."

"So your plans for the future don't involve playing on the tour forever?"

"I still want to be part of the tour." Tiernan considered how to explain a plan she hadn't fully figured out herself. She definitely didn't want the kind of relationship her parents had in the end and intended, when it was time, to work out the details of what she did want. "I should get to a point in my career when I can adjust my schedule. It won't always be necessary for me to play in every tournament. Hopefully, that'll leave time for a family. I mean, other golfers do it, don't they?"

"They do. But it's surprising to hear you talk about having a family."

"Because I'm gay?"

"No. Because you live and breathe golf."

Tiernan trailed her fingers along Elena's shoulder. "Well, I do have other interests."

Elena managed to suppress a shiver at the feel of Tiernan's fingers against her bare skin and the thought of what those other interests might be. Though she might regret it, she asked, "Like what?"

"Anything outdoors, really. Hiking, for example. I love spending a few hours along a peaceful trail. What about you?"

"Yes, I have other interests, too."

Tiernan smiled, one side of her mouth lifting slightly more

than the other. "And I would definitely like to know what those interests might be. But I was actually referring to your plans for family."

"*¡Dios mío!* My mother would have a stroke if I told her I planned to have children with my lesbian lover."

"You could do it alone."

"If I thought having kids was an option, I would probably want to be in a relationship at the time." Tiernan's fingers crept up the back of Elena's neck and into her hairline. "Tiernan," Elena moaned, unable to voice her demand that Tiernan stop.

"You could never be out to your family?" Tiernan carried on their conversation as if touching Elena had no effect on her.

"The thought has always scared me to death. It was easier to focus on my career."

"So I'm not the only one who lives and breathes golf." Tiernan scooted closer, her fingers still caressing Elena's scalp.

"I guess not." Elena let her head drop forward. "Tiernan."

"If you want me to stop, you should tell me now. I didn't invite you here to seduce you, you know."

"Then what are you doing?"

Tiernan touched her lips to the side of Elena's neck. "I can't seem to help myself. Ever since I kissed you, all I can think about is doing it again."

Despite knowing that she should stop this before it got started, Elena angled into Tiernan's embrace. Tiernan's arms came around her. Elena turned her head and their lips met and they ignited. Their kiss flared hotly as Tiernan's tongue stroked into her mouth. Elena's fingers tangled in Tiernan's hair and she pulled her closer.

Tiernan pushed Elena back, pressing her down on the loveseat, and moved over her. Elena spread her knees and Tiernan settled between them, the length of her firm body sending tiny pleasurable pulses through Elena's nervous system. Tiernan broke the kiss and rose to support her weight on one arm.

"You're so beautiful," she whispered, gazing into Elena's eyes.

Elena felt beautiful when Tiernan looked at her like that. Tiernan stroked a finger along the side of Elena's neck and down her chest to trace the plunging neckline of the dress. She teased under the fabric, tracing the swell of Elena's breast.

"Please." Elena grasped at Tiernan's hips, while lifting her own. Tiernan's fingers feathered ever closer to her nipple and she could feel it puckering in response. The weight of Tiernan's body on hers made her crave more: more pressure—more friction— more pleasure.

"I wish I could take my time with you. But I'm not sure I'm strong enough." Tiernan punctuated her words with her teeth on the underside of Elena's jaw and Elena gasped as the sharp sensation sizzled through her.

Tiernan grazed her nipple and Elena bowed her back off the sofa. She didn't want Tiernan to take her time, her body screamed with need, so much so that she almost sighed with relief when Tiernan's fingers closed firmly on her nipple.

Fleetingly, Elena thought this might not be a good idea, but Tiernan chased the notion away when she lowered her head to her breast and took her nipple in her mouth. She toyed with the firm flesh with her teeth, flicked it with her tongue, and sucked it hard. Desperate to touch skin, Elena pulled Tiernan's shirt free of her waistband and shoved her hands underneath. She raked her nails across Tiernan's back and lifted her hips, seeking pressure to try to relieve the growing ache between her thighs.

As if sensing Elena's need, Tiernan swept her hand up Elena's thigh and under the hem of her dress. She cupped her, pressing against her through her panties. Elena moaned and Tiernan slid off the sofa onto her knees on the floor. She pushed Elena's skirt up to her waist and, holding her hips, guided her closer to the edge. As she slid Elena's panties down, the soft fabric brushing her legs made Elena tremble in anticipation of Tiernan's touch.

She felt Tiernan's fingers first, gently tracing along her outer lips, separating them. Then a whispered breath as Tiernan bent her head closer. Elena buried her fingers in Tiernan's hair, and when Tiernan's tongue touched her, she tugged on the strands wrapped around her hand. Tiernan groaned.

Elena bucked beneath the onslaught of pleasure as Tiernan licked and sucked her clitoris. Her fingers tightened in Tiernan's hair and her back bowed as Tiernan drove her up, then eased her ministrations, leaving Elena clinging, trembling, to the thread of orgasm. Tiernan continued to tease her, giving her just enough to keep her grasping at the elusive string that would unravel her pleasure.

"Oh, God, Tiernan, please," Elena moaned, stumbling through the words and grasping at Tiernan's shoulders.

Tiernan held her there, shimmering on the verge, despite Elena's pleas. Elena thrust upward, trying to force Tiernan closer. Finally, Tiernan wrapped her arms around Elena's hips, and this time when she drove Elena toward climax, she didn't hold back. Elena stiffened as pleasure cascaded through her first in crashing waves, then like ripples on a pond sent outward from the impact of Tiernan's mouth and tongue.

When Elena relaxed into the cushions, panting and sated, Tiernan crawled onto the sofa beside her. She lay next to Elena and draped an arm across her stomach. Using what little energy she had, Elena turned her head and kissed Tiernan's forehead.

"Would you like to go to the bedroom?" Tiernan asked hesitantly.

Elena smiled, knowing Tiernan was looking for her regret, but she felt none. She stood, took Tiernan's hand, and led her toward the adjoining room. Once there they undressed each other and slid between two cool white sheets.

❖

Elena awoke, lying on her back with Tiernan asleep on her chest. Tiernan's cheek rested against one of Elena's breasts and her hand curled around the other. Elena smiled and rubbed her hand lightly over Tiernan's back. Her skin was warm, slightly flushed from sleep, and so soft. She trailed her hand up and down Tiernan's spine, then traced her shoulder blades.

Memories of the previous night, well into the early morning hours, rushed into her head, and Elena's body responded immediately, growing heavy with arousal.

"You'll miss that flight," Tiernan said, without opening her eyes.

Elena glanced at the bedside clock. She was supposed to be on a plane in an hour and a half. She probably had a chance to rush back to her room, throw her things into a suitcase, and make it to the airport in time. But lying there with Tiernan's body against hers, she had no desire to move. "There'll be another flight later."

"Good. Because I'm planning to make you breakfast."

"Really?"

"Yes. Cereal."

CHAPTER SEVENTEEN

I need to talk to you about Tiernan O'Shea," Cindy said, not rising from her seat behind her desk.

Elena froze four steps into Cindy's office. Hoping she could keep the tremor out of her voice, she said, "What about her?"

"We want her miked during the Open, but she's not thrilled about it."

Elena suppressed a sigh of relief. She'd been jumpy for the past week, afraid someone would find out about her and Tiernan. They'd spoken on the phone every night through the week. During that weekend's tournament, Tiernan continued to try to give Elena an interview at the end of each round, but Elena made her limit her special attention to every other day. While on the golf course, Elena acted as if nothing had changed, but later, when Tiernan came to her hotel room, she gave in to her attraction to Tiernan. She didn't know where they were going, couldn't face the consequences of her actions just yet, and Tiernan seemed content to leave things as they were, for now.

"I can ask, I guess. But I don't think she's any more likely to do it for me." The Open tournament, so named because it included professionals as well as a number of qualifying amateurs, was one of the biggest tournaments of the year. The network often tried to convince a couple of the players to wear microphones to give their viewers a different perspective.

"Maybe you could bring up the idea after one of your interviews this weekend."

"I don't know for sure I'll get—"

"Please, she gives you an interview every week. I suspect she has a bit of a crush on you since the pro-am."

"What?" Had she said something or done something to give them away? Elena was always conscious of how she looked at Tiernan while on camera or in public.

"Don't worry, honey, it's nothing to be concerned about. Just a little crush. I'm sure she knows you're straight. She won't hit on you or anything."

Elena nodded and changed the subject to work. "I'll ask her about the mic this weekend if I get a chance."

Tiernan had a full weekend, and they had already talked about when they might sneak in some time together. One morning, prior to her round, Tiernan was taking part in a photo shoot for an ad campaign urging people to vote against a proposition banning gay marriage. She talked with Elena about her plans to become involved with the ERI and some other gay and lesbian causes. And while Elena supported what those organizations were working for, Tiernan's involvement made her nervous. Whatever was going on between them was still very new, and Elena hoped any additional publicity Tiernan brought on herself didn't endanger their time together.

❖

"A win tomorrow would make four in a row for you. Are you looking to make the Open win number five?" Elena asked. She stared at Tiernan's right ear. She was quite aware that a camera was pointed at her, and she avoided eye contact because she was sure if she met Tiernan's eyes, her desires would be evident on her face. They hadn't gotten together the previous two nights because Tiernan had prior obligations. Now, standing so close to Tiernan, Elena was having difficulty keeping her mind on the interview.

"I don't want to get ahead of myself," Tiernan replied politely, with no hint of the passion from the weekend before in her voice. "There's a good bit of golf left to play tomorrow and several players still in the hunt."

"But you're going into the final round in first place."

"And that's always a great position to be in. But it's definitely not time to start thinking ahead to the Open yet."

"As the Open champion from last year, how much more pressure do you have to defend your title?"

"It's definitely a concern. The Open is always a challenge in and of itself, so Brit and I will start tackling that on Monday."

"Well, then we'll see what tomorrow brings. Good luck."

Tiernan lingered near Elena until after she'd unclipped her microphone and the cameraman turned away. She waited while Elena exchanged pleasantries with a colleague. And when they too walked away, she resisted the urge to touch Elena's arm to get her attention.

"My producer asked me to talk to you about something," Elena said when she turned back to Tiernan.

"About the microphone?"

"Yes. For the Open. It would be good publicity for you."

"I'm so sick of thinking about what's good or bad publicity."

"Your fans would probably like to hear what you're saying or thinking while you play."

"That's great as long as I'm doing well. If not, they'll get an earful." Tiernan smiled. "I'll think about it. Hey, do you like fireworks?"

"I guess so. Why?"

"Well, since today is the Fourth of July, some friends of mine who live in the area are planning to grill some burgers and set off fireworks. I thought you might want to go tonight."

"I don't think so."

"Aren't we ever going out in public?"

Elena's expression made it clear she thought Tiernan was speaking too loudly. "You know how I feel about this," she said in a hushed voice.

"I promise this is safe. It's just a few other couples. I know and trust them."

"You can't be sure that one of them won't say something to the wrong person."

"But I do. I've been hanging out with them when I'm in town for years. They've known about me the whole time, and none of them ever let it slip." Tiernan was irritated that she had to make such strong assurances, but she tried to remember how she'd felt when she had to be worried about being outed.

"You're sure no one will find out."

"Jesus, no. I'm certain."

"Okay. I've got some press to finish up here. And you have another trophy presentation. I'll meet you later."

Tiernan nodded and watched Elena walk away. Lately, she'd been looking forward to the weekends for an entirely different reason. Instead of the tournament, she had been anticipating the opportunity to spend time with Elena.

"You know, if you keep staring at that reporter like that, people may start thinking you've got a thing for her." Brit clapped a hand on Tiernan's shoulder, startling her.

Tiernan didn't catch the guilty expression before it slid across her face.

"You do," Brit exclaimed. "Oh, that's so cute. You've got a crush. I didn't know you were seriously into her. But don't you think you're reaching a little? She's pretty hot, but she might be out of your league. Not to mention probably straight." Brit kept talking, all the while laughing at Tiernan.

"Whatever you say."

"Hey, don't take it the wrong way. I mean your celebrity

more than makes up for what you're lacking in the looks area, but is that what you want a woman to be attracted to?"

"You're such a comedian." Tiernan shoved Brit's shoulder. She hadn't told her about the developments with Elena, not because she didn't trust her, but because she didn't want to hear her opinion. Brit thought she should focus on golf and probably wouldn't like hearing that she was in another relationship she had to hide.

❖

Elena walked out of the hotel and into the shadows of dusk. She passed up the valet stand and entered the parking lot, casually looking around. When she spotted the rented silver Jeep Liberty with tinted windows that Tiernan had described to her earlier, she headed that way. The Jeep was parked at the far end of the third row. As Elena approached, the window lowered.

"Ready to go." Tiernan sat in the driver's seat wearing sunglasses and a baseball cap. "Hop in."

Elena circled to the passenger side and climbed in. Tiernan reached across the console and took Elena's hand and held it for the fifteen-minute drive to the suburbs. When they arrived at the home of Tiernan's friends, she led her into the backyard and introduced her to three other couples.

The friends were welcoming and warm, and Elena felt comfortable and relaxed in the group of women. When Tiernan ventured away from her side, she came back often to check on her. The backyard was filled with music and the smell of hamburgers cooking on the grill. As night fell, someone lit tiki torches and citronella candles to ward off the mosquitoes. And when darkness had completely descended they pulled out a stash of fireworks no doubt purchased off an interstate exit in some southern state.

Elena and Tiernan sat huddled on a blanket in the grass while pyrotechnics lit up the sky above them.

"Did you enjoy yourself?" Tiernan whispered, as she wrapped her arm around Elena.

"Very much. Thank you for bringing me."

When Tiernan held her tighter, Elena turned her face up for a kiss. Tiernan's tongue slid against hers and Elena moaned and pressed closer still.

❖

Elena strode into the locker room Sunday morning, anger driving her pace, but she jerked to a halt and nearly stumbled. Tiernan lay on her stomach on a padded table in the center of the room, covered only by a towel that didn't hide anything more than her ass. An attractive brunette stood beside the table kneading Tiernan's back, and for a moment a wave of jealousy at the sight of another woman's hands on Tiernan distracted Elena. As the woman applied more pressure along Tiernan's spine, she moaned in pleasure. Her face was pressed into a hole in the top of the table and she hadn't noticed Elena yet.

When Elena balled her fist, the reason for her visit crinkled. She lurched forward and threw the tabloid on the floor under the table where Tiernan could see it. The smell of lavender drifted from Tiernan's naked body, but Elena steeled herself against both the soothing scent and the arousal that clamored to overtake her anger.

"What the hell is this?" she demanded. The image of the front page was dark but it was obviously two women embracing. In case the reader couldn't make out the faces, the large bold letters on the front spelled out Tiernan and Elena's names.

"Trash," Tiernan answered too calmly.

"You're not even mad?"

"I can't afford to get angry every time someone prints my name in a tabloid. It happens way too often."

"Not to me, it doesn't. You told me you could trust your friends."

"I do. They didn't do this. Some reporter must have followed us from the hotel." The woman moved to Tiernan's legs, massaging the backs of her thighs. "The best thing to do is—ah, God—" Tiernan groaned when strong fingers dug into her calf muscles, "just ignore it."

"I can't do that." Elena glanced down at the paper, and renewed irritation and embarrassment surged through her. "My mother saw this at the grocery store this morning."

Tiernan lifted her head and met Elena's eyes. "Did you explain to her that tabloids often print things that aren't true in order to sell papers?"

"I can't—" Elena glanced at the masseuse, and though she didn't appear to be paying any attention to them, Elena lowered her voice. "I can't lie to her."

Tiernan waved away the woman's hands and sat up. She grasped Elena's shoulders and compassion flooded her eyes. "Then tell her the truth. We can stop hiding."

"I'm not ready to do that either." The thought of telling her parents she was a lesbian terrified her. She wasn't sure they could get past their prejudices and see she was still their daughter. More likely, both her parents would disown her. Vincent's reaction was slightly more unpredictable. His generation of Latin men was a little more accepting of lesbians than of gay men.

"It seems like those are your only options."

"At this point, yes. I should have followed my instincts and stayed as far away from you as possible."

Tiernan's brows drew together and a hurt look touched her face before she pulled it back. "Now you're saying this is my fault."

"You pursued me, when you knew this wasn't what I wanted."

"You still could have refused. You're a grown woman. I think you were quite aware you were getting involved with someone who sometimes attracts media attention."

"Involved?"

"What would you call it?"

"I don't know. But whatever it is, I don't want to explain it to my mother."

Tiernan crossed the locker room, grabbed a T-shirt from a folded pile of clothes, and tugged it on. "What do you want me to do about it? I can't unprint the damn thing."

"Could we have some privacy, please?" Elena snapped as she turned toward the brunette, who still stood nearby staring at the top of her massage table. The woman began to hastily pack her belongings.

Tiernan sighed. She picked up a pair of shorts and dug a wad of folded bills out of the pocket. Pressing the money into the woman's hand she said, "Why don't you come back in a bit."

The brunette nodded, cast Elena one last look, and hurried out of the room.

"Do you really think she won't run and tell everyone she knows?" Elena glared at the door through which she had disappeared.

"Not if she wants my business again. I just paid her four times her usual rate." Tiernan took Elena by the upper arms and steered her toward a bench. "Now sit down, and let's talk about this."

Elena sat, because Tiernan's hands felt warm even through her sleeves. Tiernan released her shoulders, then, as she sat next to Elena, she captured one of her hands.

"Have you talked to your mother yet?"

"No. She called, but I was too chicken to answer the phone. She left a message."

"So, when do you anticipate speaking with her?" Tiernan rubbed her thumb over Elena's knuckles.

"I'm expected at dinner tomorrow night."

"Do you want me to go with you?"

"No," Elena said more quickly than she meant to. "No. I need to handle this alone. If I'm going to tell them the truth about myself, it should be about me and who I am, not about who I might be seeing right now." She knew confessing to her family was her only option, had known it even before she came into the locker room.

"So, we've gone from 'involved' to 'might be seeing'?"

"You know what I mean."

Tiernan nodded. "I do. Obviously, you don't think they'll react well."

"Probably not."

Her mother would likely ask her to leave their house and not return. Her father's reaction, however, was more difficult to predict these days. Beyond their general homophobia, they would be concerned about who would provide for her if she didn't have a husband. But they already worried about that now. Her parents were raised to believe that the woman's place was in the home, raising children, and the man's was to provide for the family. Vincent's wife was very submissive to him and embraced these traditional values.

Elena was their only problem child, and things were about to get a lot worse.

CHAPTER EIGHTEEN

I can't believe you didn't tell me." The first words Brit spoke to Tiernan as she walked up to the tee Monday afternoon carried an accusatory tone. They'd flown out early to do some extra preparation before the Open, and Tiernan had scheduled a tee time to get in a practice round on the front nine.

"I wasn't sure exactly what Elena and I were doing." Though Tiernan held out her hand, Brit made no move to hand her a club, so Tiernan pulled her driver from the bag herself.

"Are you sure now?"

"No."

"You know I don't think this is a good idea." Brit tossed Tiernan a ball.

"I knew you'd have reservations. That's why I didn't bring it up."

"And you don't have reservations? The woman has to be big-time closeted, right?"

Tiernan took a practice swing, then looked down the fairway. "Well, she was before this tabloid thing came out."

"How's she handling that?"

"Not well. She's having dinner with her parents tonight to talk to them about it. But she doesn't think they'll take it well."

"Would you? If your daughter was outed in the national media? And from what I gathered from Vincent, they have rather strict parents."

"Yep." Tiernan sent a ball sailing down the center of the fairway.

"So this will definitely be a test of what she really wants and what she can handle."

"It sure will." Tiernan handed over her driver and they walked toward her ball.

"I hope you know what you're doing. I only wish you happiness, of course. But I'm still mad you didn't tell me."

"I know." Tiernan hadn't expected Brit to forgive her just yet, but she would sooner or later. Brit couldn't hold a grudge. "Come on. Let's concentrate on this round. I'd love another win this weekend."

❖

The house Elena grew up in didn't look nearly as inviting as it had the last time she'd visited. Lights burned in the dining-room and living-room windows, and Elena knew she would find her mother working in the kitchen at the back of the house. But Elena sat in her car in the driveway and stared at the porch where she and her brother had played as children. Inside awaited a confrontation Elena had dreaded for the last twenty-four hours. She debated leaving without going inside, but that would only prolong the inevitable. She couldn't avoid her family forever.

The walk across the yard passed far too quickly, and sooner than she wanted, Elena was on the porch. As she stepped inside she heard laughter coming from the dining room. She had stalled as long as she could. Dinner was on the table and Elena's day of reckoning had come.

The room fell silent as Elena walked in. Her father sat in his place at the head of the table with her mother to his right. The empty seat next to her was Elena's. Vincent and his wife occupied the remaining two chairs on the other side of the table.

"Good evening," Elena said as she pulled out her chair and sat.

"Vincent, you will say grace," her mother said, without sparing Elena even a look.

They all bowed their heads obediently while he reverently murmured a prayer. When he finished, her mother began to pass platters of food. Silence permeated the room except for the sound of flatware against dishes.

For Elena, the meal was absolute torture. She vacillated between wishing someone would say something and hoping she could get through the entire meal and escape without talking. But she should have counted on her brother to stir things up.

"Where will you be traveling to this weekend, Elena?"

Elena cleared her throat. "I'll be in Pennsylvania for the Open."

"Will you be posing for any more pictures?"

"Vincent!" Her mother dropped her fork with a clatter.

"I'm just curious if I should expect more questions from the guys at work."

Elena had no response.

"That's enough, Vincent." Her father used the voice that let them know he was serious.

That's when Elena realized that, whether a conscious decision or not, her parents would choose to ignore the newspaper article if they could.

"Shit, Ma, do you know what they're saying about her?"

"You will not use that language in my house."

"Well, I don't want to go to work every day and have to explain my sister's sex life."

Suddenly, Elena was angry. Her life had become everyone else's business, and she hadn't done anything other than spend time with someone she was interested in.

"It's not just my sex life, it's my whole life," Elena blurted. Heat crept up her neck in an angry flush. "And though I know I'll have to defend it everywhere I go, I don't want to have to defend it within my own family."

"Whoa, what are you saying? It's true? You're a lesbo?"

"Of course she's not," her mother said.

"Mama—"

"No. It's unacceptable. No daughter of mine would be a pervert."

Elena flinched. Her mother's expression was unforgiving.

"I'm sorry if it hurts you or disappoints you. But it's true. I am a lesbian. And I'm currently in a relationship with Tiernan O'Shea."

"That girl who isn't Catholic?" her father asked.

Vincent snickered and Elena would have laughed if her heart hadn't already been in her throat. Her mother refused to look at her, and the jury was still out on her father's reaction, but she suspected he would side with her mother.

Without another word, her mother stood and left the room. Though Elena had been preparing herself all day for just this reaction, it hurt. Tears stung her eyes. Vincent and his wife followed her mother, leaving Elena sitting at the table with only her father.

"Papa," Elena began, but she didn't know what to say. She had to push aside the instinct to say she was sorry. If she started apologizing now she would be doing so for the rest of her life.

"You are my daughter. That will not change. But I cannot stand against your mother on this." Pain was evident in his eyes.

"What should I do?" Elena swiped at the tears that spilled down her cheek.

"Give her time."

It wasn't the answer Elena wanted, but it was the best she would get. When she left her parents' house a few minutes later, she wondered how long it would be before she was welcome there again.

❖

Elena lay alone in the dark on her bed, knowing the phone would ring any minute. Tiernan had promised to call and check on her this evening. But Elena wasn't sure she wanted to talk to anyone. Her predictable life had changed so much in such a short time. Only a few weeks ago her biggest concern was getting work on the pro tour.

Now, she'd just alienated her entire family and thrust herself into the tabloid spotlight. She didn't worry anymore how the revelation would impact her job. The network would probably love the publicity that having one of their on-air personalities tied to an athlete would bring.

Did she want to be "tied" to Tiernan? She pulled the blanket higher under her chin, fear coiling in her stomach as she realized that she did. Telling her family the truth had been the beginning of living a more honest life. But now she needed to examine whether she could see herself in a relationship with Tiernan, long-term.

Tiernan was more than the superficial one-dimensional woman Elena had originally pegged her as. She'd opened up to Elena about her own family dramas. After having lost her father, Tiernan had gone against her mother's wishes and quit school to pursue golf, because that's how she needed to honor her father's memory.

In a short time, Tiernan had come to mean a lot to her. When Tiernan touched her, she experienced all the things she'd never thought she would feel—never thought existed. Tiernan excited her and made her feel beautiful and alive. She didn't think about schedules or timelines, only the pleasure of being with Tiernan. Although there were plenty of sparks between them, Elena wasn't just physically attracted to Tiernan; she was also drawn to her vulnerability and strength. She'd seen a change in Tiernan in the time she'd known her—a renewed passion for golf as well as for life. Though Tiernan was still serious about her career, she no longer devoted every minute to training. She kept her commitments and worked hard, but when she and Elena spent time together, she remained present and attentive to Elena.

The question seemed to be not whether Elena wanted to take

a chance with Tiernan, but whether she was brave enough to deal with the scrutiny.

She was saved from further examining her own makeup when the phone rang.

"How did it go?" Tiernan asked immediately.

"Not great." Elena sighed, fighting tears for the second time today. But hearing Tiernan's voice over the phone line brought her a measure of comfort. "My mother isn't speaking to me. My brother thinks my life is a disastrous joke. And my father won't stick up for me."

"I'm sorry."

Elena sobbed, unable to hold onto the heartache she'd been fighting since visiting her parents' home. "What are you sorry about?"

"For getting you wrapped up in my messy life."

"I think you pointed out that was my decision." Elena rolled to her back and stretched out. She'd been lying there since she got home. For a little while she'd been curled into a fetal position, hoping it would ease the ache in her stomach. She felt sick and nauseated since leaving her parents' home.

"All the same, I shouldn't have talked you into going to that party."

"Please, I don't need your guilt on my conscience, too. I hate the media attention and I hate what it'll do to my family. But the end result is the same. I need to live my life in a way that will make me happy, without hiding from who I am. I'm not there yet. But I guess this is the road to that place."

"I wish I were there with you instead of here," Tiernan said.

"Yeah? If you were, what would you do?"

"Hold you and tell you how wonderful you are. And how if your family has any sense they'll come around, because they'll realize what they'll miss by not having you in their lives."

Tiernan's response was surprisingly in line with what Elena needed to hear, but she still wasn't feeling particularly optimistic.

"In a perfect world, maybe. But for now all I can say is, we'll see."

"I'm here, if you need anything in the meantime."

"I know. I think I'll try to get some sleep. Practice well tomorrow and I'll see you in a couple of days."

❖

Two days later, Elena still hadn't heard from anyone in her family. But she packed her things and boarded a plane to Pennsylvania because that's what her schedule indicated and she didn't know what else to do. The plane ride was long and turbulent, and by the time they landed in Allentown she was more than ready to be on the ground.

She fell into the crowd of people exiting her plane, and they moved down the hallway from the gate to the terminal like a herd of animals. Every so often someone in a hurry to get to baggage claim and stand around would break out of the pack and power walk ahead. They bottlenecked at the escalator and filed onto the moving stairs one by one.

As Elena rode down, she saw a cluster of people waiting in the baggage area. But she immediately recognized one face in the crowd. Tiernan stepped forward as Elena got off the escalator. She pulled Elena in for a hug, then released her just as quickly.

"What are you doing here? Shouldn't you be practicing?"

"There's plenty of time for practice. Besides, if I'm not ready now, I'll never be. So I'm picking you up from the airport, then I'm taking you back to our hotel room."

"Our room?"

Tiernan shrugged. "I took a chance. You still have your room reserved if you want to use it. But I'd like you to stay with me."

"Tiernan, maybe this is all too fast, or too complicated."

"Elena, being away from you when I know you're having a hard time with all this has been killing me. I've wanted nothing more than to be with you and help you sort it all out. But it's your call. I'm telling you what I'm offering and you're welcome to take it or refuse it." Tiernan brushed her hand down the outside of Elena's arm and encircled her wrist.

"What are you offering?"

"A relationship. One that includes lots of travel. But on the upside, I promise to take time off to spend with you whenever we're in the same city. I've been a ton of places I've never actually seen, and I'd like to do that with you. It's also an honest and open relationship. I need to tell you that now. I'm all about having privacy, but I won't hide or deny you. I've done that for too long and I don't want to do it again. I'm offering you a partnership with someone who adores you—who loves you."

Elena's heart tripped at Tiernan's words, but she kept her expression neutral. "Those are your terms?"

"Well, there is one more thing."

"Yes."

"I've been invited to be the keynote speaker at the ERI dinner next week. I'd like you to accompany me."

"So, we would be officially confirming the tabloid reports."

"That's an unfortunate side effect, yes. But, actually, I just need a date, and there's no one I'd rather go with."

"Then I accept. The date and your terms."

"Even if your family never comes around?"

"Yes. I can't live as who they want me to be. I have dreams of my own, and one of them includes having someone to share my life with."

"You know, Brit told me in Orlando that she thought we make a good match."

"I think she was talking about golf."

"Maybe. But she was more right than she knew."

About the Author

Erin Dutton often draws inspiration for her books from her adopted home in Nashville. Often, the things she loves can be found in her stories—from her hobbies and interests to themes involving love and family.

Her previous novels include five romances: *Sequestered Hearts*, *Fully Involved*, *A Place to Rest*, *Designed For Love*, and *Point of Ignition*. She is also a contributor to *Erotic Interludes 5: Road Games*, and *Romantic Interludes* 1& 2 from Bold Strokes Books.

Books Available From Bold Strokes Books

The Pleasure Set by Lisa Girolami. Laney DeGraff, a successful president of a family-owned bank on Rodeo Drive, finds her comfortable life taking a turn toward danger when Theresa Aguilar, a sleek, sexy lawyer, invites her to join an exclusive, secret group of powerful, alluring women. (978-1-60282-144-6)

A Perfect Match by Erin Dutton. The exciting world of pro golf forms the backdrop for a fast-paced, sexy romance. (978-1-60282-145-3)

Truths by Rebecca S. Buck. Two women separated by two hundred years are connected by fate and love. (978-1-60282-146-0)

Father Knows Best by Lynda Sandoval. High school juniors and best friends Lila Moreno, Meryl Morganstern, and Caressa Thibodoux plan to make the most of the summer before senior year. What they discover that amazing summer about girl power, growing up, and trusting friends and family more than prepares them to tackle that all-important senior year! (978-1-60282-147-7)

In Pursuit of Justice by Radclyffe. In the dynamic double sequel to *Shield of Justice* and *A Matter of Trust*, Det. Sgt. Rebecca Frye joins forces with enigmatic computer consultant J.T. Sloan to crack an Internet child pornography ring. (978-1-60282-147-4)

The Midnight Hunt by L.L. Raand. Medic Drake McKennan takes a chance and loses, and her life will never be the same—because when she wakes up after surviving a life-threatening illness, she is no longer human. (978-1-60282-140-8)

Long Shot by D. Jackson Leigh. Love isn't safe, which is exactly why equine veterinarian Tory Greyson wants no part of it—until Leah Montgomery and a horse that won't give up convince her otherwise. (978-1-60282-141-5)

In Medias Res by Yolanda Wallace. Sydney has forgotten her entire life, and the one woman who holds the key to her memory, and her heart, doesn't want to be found. (978-1-60282-142-2)

Awakening to Sunlight by Lindsey Stone. Neither Judith or Lizzy is looking for companionship, and certainly not love—but when their lives become entangled, they discover both. (978-1-60282-143-9)

Fever by VK Powell. Hired gun Zakaria Chambers is hired to provide a simple escort service to philanthropist Sara Ambrosini, but nothing is as simple as it seems, especially love. (978-1-60282-135-4)

High Risk by JLee Meyer. Can actress Kate Hoffman really risk all she's worked for to take a chance on love? Or is it already too late? (978-1-60282-136-1)

Missing Lynx by Kim Baldwin and Xenia Alexiou. On the trail of a notorious serial killer, Elite Operative Lynx's growing attraction to a mysterious mercenary could be her path to love—or to death. (978-1-60282-137-8)

Spanking New by Clifford Henderson. A poignant, hilarious, unforgettable look at life, love, gender, and the essence of what makes us who we are. (978-1-60282-138-5)

Magic of the Heart by C.J. Harte. CEO Susan Hettinger and wild, impulsive rock star M.J. Carson couldn't be more different if they tried—but opposites attract in ways neither woman can resist. (978-1-60282-131-6)

Ambereye by Gill McKnight. Jolie Garoul is falling in love with her assistant. The big problem is, Jolie is a werewolf. (978-1-60282-132-3)

Collision Course by C.P. Rowlands. Tragedy leaves Brie O'Malley and Jordan Carter fearful and alone. Can they find the courage to take a second chance on love? (978-1-60282-133-0)

Mephisto Aria by Justine Saracen. Opera singer Katherina Marov's destiny may be to repeat the mistakes of her father when she becomes involved in a dangerous love affair. (978-1-60282-134-7)

Battle Scars by Meghan O'Brien. Returning Iraq war veteran Ray McKenna struggles with the battle scars that can only be healed by love. (978-1-60282-129-3)

Chaps by Jove Belle. Eden Metcalf wants nothing more than to flee from her troubled past and travel the open road—until she runs into rancher Brandi Cornwell. (978-1-60282-127-9)

Lightbearer by John Caruso. Lucifer dares to question the premise of creation itself and reveals that sin may be all that stands between us and living hell. (978-1-60282-130-9)

The Seeker by Ronica Black. FBI profiler Kennedy Scott battles ghosts from her past, deadly obsession, and the evil that haunts her. (978-1-60282-128-6)

Power Play by Julie Cannon. Businesswomen Tate Monroe and Victoria Sosa are at odds in the boardroom, but not in the bedroom. (978-1-60282-125-5)

The Remarkable Journey of Miss Tranby Quirke by Elizabeth Ridley. When love enters Tranby's life in the form of a beautiful nineteen-year-old student, Lysette McDonald, she embarks on the most remarkable journey of all. (978-1-60282-126-2)

Returning Tides by Radclyffe. Insurance investigator Ashley Walker faces more than a dangerous opponent when she returns to the town, and the woman, she left behind. (978-1-60282-123-1)

Veritas by Anne Laughlin. When the hallowed halls of academia become the stage for murder, newly appointed Dean Beth Ellis's search for the truth leads her to unexpected discoveries about her own heart. (978-1-60282-124-8)

The Pleasure Planner by Larkin Rose. Pleasure purveyor Bree Hendricks treats love like a commodity until Logan Delaney makes Bree the client in her own game. (978-1-60282-121-7)

everafter by Nell Stark and Trinity Tam. Valentine Darrow is bitten by a vampire on her way to propose to her lover Alexa Newland, and their lives and love are placed in mortal jeopardy. (978-1-60282-119-4)

Summer Winds by Andrews & Austin. When Maggie Turner hires a ranch hand to help work her thousand acres, she never expects to be attracted to the very young, very female Cash Tate. (978-1-60282-120-0)

Beggar of Love by Lee Lynch. Jefferson is the lover every woman wants to be—or to have. A revealing saga of lesbian sexuality. (978-1-60282-122-4)

The Seduction of Moxie by Colette Moody. When 1930s Broadway actress Violet London meets speakeasy singer Moxie Valette, she is instantly attracted and her Hollywood trip takes an unexpected turn. (978-1-60282-114-9)

Goldenseal by Gill McKnight. When Amy Fortune returns to her childhood home, she discovers something sinister in the air—but is former lover Leone Garoul stalking her or protecting her? (978-1-60282-115-6)

Romantic Interludes 2: Secrets edited by Radclyffe and Stacia Seaman. An anthology of sensual lesbian love stories: passion, surprises, and secret desires. (978-1-60282-116-3)

Femme Noir by Clara Nipper. Nora Delaney meets her match in Max Abbott, a sex-crazed dame who may or may not have the information Nora needs to solve a murder—but can she contain her lust for Max long enough to find out? (978-1-60282-117-0)

The Reluctant Daughter by Lesléa Newman. Heartwarming, heartbreaking, and ultimately triumphant—the story every daughter recognizes of the lifelong struggle for our mothers to really see us. (978-1-60282-118-7)

Erosistible by Gill McKnight. When Win Martin arrives at a luxurious Greek hotel for a much-anticipated week of sun and sex with her new girlfriend, she is stunned to find her ex-girlfriend, Benny, is the proprietor. Aeros Ebook. (978-1-60282-134-7)

Looking Glass Lives by Felice Picano. Cousins Roger and Alistair become lifelong friends and discover their sexuality amidst the backdrop of twentieth-century gay culture. (978-1-60282-089-0)

Breaking the Ice by Kim Baldwin. Nothing is easy about life above the Arctic Circle—except, perhaps, falling in love. At least that's what pilot Bryson Faulkner hopes when she meets Karla Edwards. (978-1-60282-087-6)

It Should Be a Crime by Carsen Taite. Two women fulfill their mutual desire with a night of passion, neither expecting more until law professor Morgan Bradley and student Parker Casey meet again…in the classroom. (978-1-60282-086-9)

Rough Trade edited by Todd Gregory. Top male erotica writers pen their own hot, sexy versions of the term "rough trade," producing some of the hottest, nastiest, and most dangerous fiction ever published. (978-1-60282-092-0)

The High Priest and the Idol by Jane Fletcher. Jemeryl and Tevi's relationship is put to the test when the Guardian sends Jemeryl on a mission that puts her not only in harm's way, but back into the sights of a previous lover. (978-1-60282-085-2)

Point of Ignition by Erin Dutton. Amid a blaze that threatens to consume them both, firefighter Kate Chambers and property owner Alexi Clark redefine love and trust. (978-1-60282-084-5)